THE LOVE PAYOFF

AMELIA ADDLER

ANJ
Press

THE LOVE PAYOFF

ANJ Press, First edition. July 2023.

Written by Amelia Addler.

Cover design by CrocoDesigns

To my family, with love

CHAPTER ONE

Anna

Let's agree that accepting a marriage proposal is a dangerous thing to do, and accepting one from a stranger is marginally more dangerous.

Okay, fine. The stranger part increases the risk more than marginally. Maybe astronomically. Who's measuring these things, anyway?

I could've ended up being the measurement, the warning, the headline you saw on the local news. "She agreed to marry the man hours after he approached her in the Madison University dining hall."

It's never good when you can envision a newscaster announcing the dumb thing you did.

In my defense, I *really* needed the money, and it wasn't an actual marriage. It was only an engagement, and a fake one at that. I wouldn't fake an entire marriage. I'm not an animal. My mom raised me to be a lady, always telling me I needed to settle down and be a good little wife.

Ha! Just kidding.

My mom is actually the Polish immigrant version of George Bailey in the 1946 classic *It's a Wonderful Life*. Not because she ran a bank, or fell into an icy river, or had an angel intervene to save her life (that we know of – she talks about angels a lot, but we assume that's the Pope's influence).

No, my mother is George Bailey in the moment when he comes home on Christmas, broke and hopeless, and yells out "Why did we have to go and have all these kids?"

Like George, my mom had four kids, but unlike George, her neighbors didn't all pull together to give her a pile of cash when times got tough. She had to go out and make that money by herself.

(Well, not *entirely* by herself. My dad wasn't a deadbeat or anything. We all tend to take him and his jovial attitude for granted, though).

In Poland, my mom was nearly finished with medical school when she got the chance to come to America.

America! Leaving communist-controlled Poland for *America!*

She took the chance, and while it was the right choice, she didn't get to be a doctor. She ended up being a maid.

That's life.

"Zuzia," she'd say, dragging a vacuum and forcing a smile at whatever client was waving us off. "You can't have it all. That is a trick on women. You can *do* it all, but you can't *have* it all."

I nodded dutifully, having little idea of the controversy surrounding the phrase "have it all," while agreeing whole-heartedly with whatever she said.

"Don't get married," she told me. "Don't have kids. You live your own life. You will be a *doctor!*"

She always whispered the word *doctor*, as though she were afraid if she said it too loud, someone would snatch it out of my hand and replace it with a bucket full of rags.

I listened to her, like I (almost) always do. I didn't get married. I didn't have kids.

I got a doctorate – in engineering, not medicine. It's almost as useful, as long as you're building a plane and not, for example, having a heart attack on one.

Truly, my life was going more or less according to plan. Until *he* showed up.

"Suzanna Makowski?"

I startled, looking up from my wilted salad. My mind was miles away, in a jail cell, not on the rotting leaves in front of me.

"Yes?"

"Can I sit?"

He stared at me with unlaughing, clear blue eyes and a perfectly straight mouth.

My first thought was that I was in trouble, or that I'd committed some sort of social faux pas. A normal person might rush to correct whatever they'd done, but not me. By this stage of my life, I'd embarrassed myself so many times that it took something truly awful to make me pause.

Are you jealous? Don't be. I'll tell you the trick – start embarrassing yourself at a young age, and don't stop until you are so comfortable being uncomfortable that the only sense of belonging is being outside of it all. *Unbelonging*.

That's me. An awkward, clumsy young woman who, in the first grade, showed up to school dressed in a purple velour tracksuit (courtesy of my mom) and a lunch box filled with pickles and foot-long smoked sausages (Polish kabanosy, rush-packed by my dad).

It doesn't take much to become an "other," and that was the day the other kids started calling me "weenie face."

Are you horrified? Do you know what happens to a six-year-old who gets called weenie face?

I'll tell you what happens. She becomes a thirty-year-old woman who, when approached by a handsome stranger, tries to send him off with "Why don't you pick one of the empty tables instead?"

He ignored my suggestion and pulled out a chair. I sighed, sitting back to get a better look at him.

Despite his stern face, he wasn't dressed like anyone in authority. He wore a blue bomber jacket and a gray t-shirt, tight enough that I could make out his lean muscles beneath.

Not that I was looking at his muscles. They just happened to be there.

His hair was black, so black that it seemed to absorb light, like a raven's feathers. It was neat at the sides but longer at the top, with a disheveled-but-dashing appearance that suggested he'd spent hours applying product to get it to fall in *just* the right, vain way.

He ran a hand through his hair and tousled the strands, immediately disproving my vanity theory.

Was he a student? I was supposed to be nice to students.

The dark stubble peppering his pale skin and the fine wrinkles near the corners of his eyes suggested no.

I was familiar with wrinkles. I'd started battling my own that year. Before then, I foolishly thought I wasn't old enough for wrinkles.

Oh, to be young.

His gaze settled on me, the bright blue of his eyes a stark contrast to his black eyelashes. He had high cheekbones and an expression of cool dismissal.

Maybe he was a vampire?

(I'll be honest, I read *Twilight* once, and while I will deny this in any social setting or court of law, I enjoyed it.)

"I'm Leo." He motioned to the ID hanging from his neck that read **STAFF.**

Vampires didn't wear lanyards. So much for that theory.

I set my fork down. It seemed I had no choice but to be nice. "You can call me Anna. Are you new to Madison University?"

He nodded. "I just signed on to teach in the school of fine arts."

"I'm with engineering."

"I know."

I raised an eyebrow and he hesitated, adding, "Someone said you might be able to help me."

"I'm not very artistic," I said, resuming my salad foraging, "but what's up?"

"Do you speak Polish?"

That was a complicated question. "Who's asking?"

"Well...me." He stared, eyes fixed, not even the hint of a smile on his face.

Not one to joke around. "My mom will tell you my Polish is beautiful. My uncle says I sound like a baby, and my grandma will tell you it's best I stick to English."

He shifted in his seat. "*Troszkę?*"

A little bit?

I smiled, replying in Polish. "*Yes. And you?*"

He shook his head. "Barely. My mother is Polish, though."

"It was my first language, but it's fallen by the wayside. I can carry a conversation, but I can't, like, translate a doctor's visit for you. I don't know those words, and you should probably keep that information personal, because I am not bound by HIPAA."

He pulled back. "Are you not good at keeping secrets?"

What a question. "Depends on the secret, I guess? If you wired a bunch of money to a Polish prince, then yes, I'm going to tell everyone, and we're going to make fun of you."

"It's nothing like that." He leaned in, placing his hands on the table. "I have a proposition for you."

"Yeah?" I pushed the salad away. It had been a mistake to try to salvage anything from the "best intentions" drawer in my fridge. That lettuce should've gone right in the trash. I could feel the food poisoning already, bubbling up and scolding me for being too lazy to go to the store and too cheap to pay for lunch. "Is it an exciting investment opportunity?"

"Sort of." His eyes flitted down to the salad for a moment, then back to me. "I'd like you to be my fiancée."

CHAPTER TWO

Leo

She erupted into a cackling laugh, tossing her head back and sending her blonde hair bouncing in a jolly sort of way.

I almost hadn't recognized her at first. Her lab's website had a picture of her squinting out from behind large black glasses. In it, she looked like a stock image of a female scientist – pretty but serious. Very serious.

She was even prettier today, the sunlight illuminating the blonde and brown tones in her hair, her eyes a clear and deep caramel flecked with bits of gold. She was no less serious, and definitely believable for a fiancée.

A smile lingered at the corners of her eyes before slowly fading. "I'm sorry. What?" she asked. "Is this an art project?"

I shifted in my seat. "No."

"A social experiment, then?" She turned, looking over her shoulder. "Are there cameras somewhere?"

"You wouldn't have to actually marry me," I said, trying to mentally run through the bullet points I'd written out the night before. "And it would only be for a few months."

If all went well, that is... but now wasn't the time to talk details.

"Oh, is that all?" She nodded solemnly, lifting a grey lunchbox from the seat beside her. "What an exciting opportunity."

"I can tell you about – "

She cut me off. "Unfortunately, I'm already pretending to be *another* guy's fiancée. It's a buyer's market these days—inflation and all—but thanks so much. Good luck."

Tucking the glass salad container into her bag, she stood up and turned.

"This isn't a prank." I reached into my pocket and pulled out an envelope. "I can pay you."

She narrowed her eyes. "If you're looking for the mail order bride department, you're going to want to take a left at the bathrooms and walk until you see the sign for the time machine."

I had to bite my lip to hide my smile. Though I expected an awkward conversation, I hadn't expected open hostility. "I have ten thousand dollars here."

She stopped, looked down at the envelope, then up at me. "For what?"

"For you to consider my proposal."

"Usually men present the initial gift in the form of a ring."

"You can buy whatever you want." I thrust the envelope toward her. "A ring, ten rings. Whatever."

She eyed the envelope for a moment. "Ten thousand dollars?"

"Ten thousand dollars."

I watched as she reached forward and delicately splayed the envelope open, peering inside. It didn't look like much, I'll admit, but that's what ten grand in hundreds was.

I'd gotten her attention, at least, and it seemed my calculations were correct. Ten thousand was a lot to a post doc. Especially one whose brother had recently catapulted himself to the forefront of the entire institution's gossip train, and whose bail was set at ten thousand exactly.

I cleared my throat. "I know this is strange, but I don't want anything weird from you."

"Is this like a *Water for Elephants* deal?"

I frowned. "What's a *Water for Elephants* deal?"

"You need me to speak Polish to the elephant so it'll perform for your circus?"

I couldn't stop myself this time. I let out a laugh. "What?"

"It's a movie. Actually, it was a book first, but the movie is really good too. You should watch it."

"Okay." I shrugged. "I will."

Anna fidgeted, scratching her nose, then tapped the envelope on the table. "I don't understand why you need someone to do this."

"It's complicated. You wouldn't be talking to an elephant, but you'd need to talk to someone."

"In Polish?"

"Yeah." We were finally getting somewhere. "We can discuss it, get a coffee maybe?"

"I have my lab meeting." She thrust the envelope into my chest. "Sorry, this is – yeah, not for me."

I kept my hands in my coat pockets. "It's ten thousand to start, and a hundred thousand total."

She took a breath, her hand still pressing the envelope to my chest. "A hundred thousand *dollars?*"

I nodded. "My contact information is in there. Just think about it and get back to me."

Before she had a chance to say anything else, I turned and walked away.

CHAPTER THREE

Anna

D id that really happen? I felt strange, like I was the fourth-grade version of myself leaning closer to the boy I liked, but instead of telling me the secret he'd promised, he spit gum into my hair.

It was the lunchbox. It made me feel like an awkward child, once again a weenie face. I tucked it under my arm and peeked into the envelope.

Still full of cash. I sucked in a breath.

On the left side, a business card. I took it out, studying the background with the sweeping farm landscape before flipping it over: **Leo Mayakovsky**.

There was a website and email listed beneath his name. Though I *obviously* wasn't going to consider his proposition, it wouldn't hurt to get to know a bit more about him...

A voice called out behind me. "Afternoon, Anna!"

I spun, clutching the envelope to my chest. "Ernie, hey."

"I haven't been seeing you here late anymore." He smiled, pulling a trash cart behind him. "Out having fun, I hope?"

"Ha, yeah, maybe." For the past two years, it had been a nightly ritual for Ernie to stop by my desk as he emptied the trash cans, have a chat, and give me a piece of candy. For a while it was Werther's, then Bazooka gum for a dark period, and most recently, Smarties.

"Got yourself a boyfriend?" he asked, a twinkle in his eye.

I shoved the envelope into my lunchbox and replied, "Oh, yeah. I'm practically married!"

He laughed, and I laughed, and while I told myself I would only see Leo again to return the money, I also knew I was absolutely going to keep it.

Like all irrational decisions, it would just take a while to accept.

Back in lab, I managed to get to my desk without having to talk to anyone. It wasn't located in the most private spot – some might call it a desk in a hallway – but I could normally work undisturbed.

Still, where was I going to stash all this money? Anyone walking by could rummage through my desk and find it. I didn't have a key to lock it inside one of the drawers. Any meaningful accessories went missing years ago, way back when the desk was dragged into this lab during the height of disco.

One of the grad students walked past and I nodded a hello, hunching over my lunchbox like I was harboring nuclear secrets. Sweat gathered on my forehead. I wiped it away.

This was worse than the last time I had gone to Poland and my aunt had insisted on stuffing my suitcase with smoked meats and dried mushrooms.

Did you know you're not supposed to smuggle meat and fungi into the country, no matter how much your aunt insists your dad needs to try them? And do you know how hard it is not to attract the drug-sniffing airport dogs when you've got a suitcase *full of sausages?*

This envelope was worse than the sausages. Definitely worse.

After much debate, I pulled my purse out of the desk drawer where it lived, secured the strap across my chest, and then, and *only* then, did I reveal the envelope and zip it inside.

Ten *thousand* dollars. He'd handed it over like it was nothing. How much money did this guy have? Was it all an act? Was this drug money? Or was he selling smoked meats on the side, like some kind of sausage kingpin?

It was time to look him up. At first I considered going to his website, but that was too easy. That was where he *wanted* me to look, where he'd act like he had a legitimate sausage business and not like he smuggled ketamine-filled kielbasa across the border.

I was onto him. I searched his name online, like a true detective, and the first result was a news story: **Mayakovsky portrait fetches $260,000 at auction.**

I'll admit, my mouth popped open like one of the only pieces of art my family ever owned, a bass fish that sang "Don't Worry Be Happy" when you pushed a button.

I skimmed the news story. There were no pictures of the artist, though the article did say he was "a fixture in SoHo nightlife" and was "known for his photorealistic portraits with a touch of whimsy."

The portrait in question was shown at the bottom of the article. It was of a girl on horseback, a glint in her eye and a half smile at the corner of her mouth. The sky surrounding her was light and airy, filled with clouds. Wings were reflected in her iris.

It looked nice, but how was it *a quarter of a million* nice?

I stared at the painting, and after a minute, I saw that one of the clouds was faintly shaped like a castle.

Hm. Cute, I guess.

"Mayakovsky," the article went on to say, "originally made the painting for Utica Children's Hospital. However, after a flurry of interest, administrators made the decision to auction the painting for funding."

Oh. That was a bit more wholesome than I'd suspected.

I went back to the search and clicked on a blog post about a gallery opening. There was a picture of Leo there, holding a glass of champagne and dressed in a black t-shirt. He was sort of smiling, but not really, and the woman next to him was in stilettos and a dress that fit like a red potato sack.

You know you're dealing with *really* rich people when they dress like that. Or maybe I just don't get fashion.

Growing up poor, the last thing I wanted to do was *look* poor, and a potato sack dress definitely looked poor. Honestly, I didn't even like wearing sweatpants in the privacy of my own home, for fear that whatever money I'd gotten into my bank account would see me and try to escape to some woman who deserved it and wore suits at all times.

Ahem. Ten *thousand* dollars! Even with my best efforts over the past decade, I only had three thousand dollars in my savings. (Two thousand nine hundred and eighty-four, but who's counting?)

I closed the search and sat back, the chair creaking beneath my weight. It seemed true, at least, that Leo had money. Fancy people money. Wear a t-shirt to a glamorous New York City event money.

If he was so fabulous, why did he need a fake fiancée? And why did he want it to be *me?* Why not the potato sack lady, or a friend, or someone he knew?

It didn't seem real, and yet he'd handed me, a perfect stranger, all that money. How'd he know I wouldn't just run off with it?

He must've thought I was greedy, that I'd come back for the rest.

I scoffed. As it happened, greed wasn't my problem. If it were, I wouldn't have gotten a PhD in hydraulic engineering, only to work as a postdoc for four years.

Even still, I was getting by just fine on my salary. I didn't need more. Not for myself. I needed it for Frankie.

Frankie's the youngest in my family, born when I was eleven. He was an angel of a baby, with exquisitely round cheeks, ever-bursting with smiles and giggles, and a head of curly blond hair.

When my mom brought him home, I was in heaven. It was like having a real-life baby doll. I lugged him around in his stroller, insisted on filing his nails (because I'd decided my mom did it wrong), and became an expert in diaper rash, bubble baths, and story time.

He was unbelievably perfect – until he wasn't. The bruising started when he was three, along with the swelling, and the tiredness, and fear.

Leukemia.

He got treatment, and he survived. The rest of us survived, too, but barely.

Frankie is twenty now, healthy as can be, but he'd picked up a new problem. For the previous two weeks he'd been stuck in the Dane County jail, unable to make his ten-thousand-dollar cash bail.

He's not a criminal. He's innocent! I couldn't lead with the whole jail thing, because as soon as you mention a crime, that's all anyone can see – a criminal.

My baby brother isn't a criminal. He's a *baby*. Okay, he's not a baby anymore, but he's a mischievous little dude who happens to have *incredibly* stupid friends. They love getting him into trouble, but this time, he had nothing to do with it.

Really.

My parents were trying to find out if they could take a third mortgage on their house to hire a good attorney for him, but now it seemed like a solution had dropped into my lap.

"Anna?"

I jolted from my daze and spotted my mentor and boss, Carl, down the hall with a mug of coffee.

"Hey! Sorry, I was lost in thought."

"No problem. Lab meeting's canceled. I wasn't sure if you'd seen."

I shook my head. "Hadn't been in my email yet."

"I'm glad you're here. I've got something exciting to talk to you about."

I doubted it could be as exciting as the scheme I was currently talking myself into, but I decided to hear him out anyway. "Lay it on me."

"One of the local news channels asked if we could comment on a new project proposed for Lake Michigan."

"What project?"

He made a face. "Not sure, but they need someone to comment on the fluid mechanics involved, and I thought it would be a fantastic chance to showcase your talents."

"You mean *on* the news?"

Carl nodded. "It's fun, don't you think?"

"I don't know." I leaned back and crossed my arms. "I'm not the most eloquent speaker."

"That's not true! Your talk on streamflow variability was *well* praised."

Dear, sweet Carl and his unfaltering faith in me.

We bickered back and forth for half an hour. His argument was that it would look good for the university, and thus improve my chances of landing my dream position as a tenure-track professor.

"What if I say something dumb?" I countered.

He thought on this for a moment. "If you sense yourself getting close to saying anything dumb, then stop and don't say that thing."

We laughed, and ultimately I agreed to do the show. It was mainly a distraction, because just before I left to go downtown

I sent Leo an email. I didn't want to be stuck waiting around for his response.

I kept it brief. "I'd like to talk. Where can we meet?"

• • •

I'd never been to a news station before, and the process started off disappointingly boring. First, I checked in with security in the lobby of the building. The guard stuck a "visitor" sticker on my jacket, then sent me up to the eleventh floor to be greeted by an intern.

She led me to a small room with a chair and a brightly-lit mirror (like in the movies!). I asked her what exactly they wanted me to comment on, but she couldn't answer.

"I think it's the pipeline story, but I'm not sure. I can check?"

Since Carl hadn't been entirely sure, either, my fear of making a fool of myself increased. "I guess I'll wait here."

"Make yourself at home!"

A makeup woman stopped by and offered to help me with how my face looked.

She didn't put it that way, of course, but that was what she meant. I agreed, and she skillfully applied a large amount of foundation, eyeshadow, and lipstick.

"It'll look natural on camera," she said before leaving me to stare at my clownish red lips in the mirror.

After half an hour, the intern returned and confirmed I was to comment on "the pipeline story."

"What kind of pipeline is it?" I asked.

She bit her lip. "Let me get one of the presenters."

This was when none other than Madison's finest newscaster, Dolly Figs, came in and hugged me.

The Dolly Figs!

Yes, her name is actually Dolly Figs, and yes, she's a local legend. For years growing up, I'd hear, "Dolly said the storm could knock out the power!" or "Dolly doesn't think skateboarding is safe," as though Dolly were an old friend of my parents, not the woman on the evening news.

She came in and gave me a hug, and she smelled *so* nice, and we took a picture, all while she told me about the story we would discuss on camera.

I was too starstruck to fully understand what she was saying, but there was a plan to build a pipeline to pull water from Lake Michigan...or something.

"We'll ask you some questions about feasibility and environmental impact, if that works for you?"

"Sure," I said, starry-eyed. "I can talk about whatever you want!"

And so, with hope in my heart and love in my eyes, I sat in front of a green screen, thirty feet away from Dolly, mic'd and eager to make her proud.

They counted down and she zeroed in on the camera in front of her.

"Good evening, Madison, and welcome to Issues at Eleven. Drought is a real problem for much of the country," she began, her voice even and newscaster stern. "A new company has plans to solve that, and the solution may surprise you. Today I've got the CEO of Ship2O, Ken Fielding, and Suzanna Makowski, an engineering expert in hydrology from Madison University. Welcome."

The screen in front of me cut to a man with short, brown hair and a brilliant white smile. "Thanks for having me, Dolly."

A guy with a clipboard and a headset pointed at me and I flashed a smile, but before I could say anything, Ken started talking.

"We're very excited to bring this project to Wisconsin's shores."

"Tell us more about what Ship2O does," Dolly said with a nod.

"At Ship2O, we're going to solve the water crisis in the west with a new pipeline that will pull water from Lake Michigan and transport it as far as California."

A pipeline to California? That was...impossible.

I stiffened in my seat.

"Ken," Dolly continued, "Some critics fear that taking water from the Great Lakes will jeopardize our local water supply. What do you say to those critics?"

"I say they should stop being so greedy with their water!" He laughed. "Trust me, Dolly. I know what I'm doing."

"It looks like Suzanna might have some doubts," Dolly said with a laugh.

Shoot. I didn't realize my face had twisted into a scowl.

I took a breath and forced a neutral expression. "It's an interesting proposition, to be sure."

"Suzanna, can you tell us a bit about your background?"

I should've told her to call me Anna. It was only a matter of time before someone made an "Oh Suzanna!" joke.

Whatever. I needed to focus on not saying anything dumb. That was my mission. I could do it.

"Sure." I nodded. "I have a PhD in engineering with a focus on hydrology and fluid dynamics. In my last position, my research focused solely on drought and rainwater management."

"What do you think about this pipeline?" Dolly asked.

Don't say anything stupid. Don't say anything stupid. "This is not a new idea. There have been a number of proposed cross-country water pipelines, as well as pipelines from glaciers, but none of them have proved to be feasible. The cost to move that much water is astronomical, and like you said, there are concerns about depleting the local water supply."

Ken shook his head. "Luckily, I'm not someone who lets naysayers get in the way of a great idea."

I couldn't even wrap my head around how wrong and dumb this was. "It's not naysayers getting in the way. It's physics. The energy costs to move that much water are—"

He cut me off. "We're innovators. We're going to make the impossible possible."

I frowned. "That's a catchy phrase, but what do you have behind it?"

"Let's be honest," he said, his smile widening. "If the ivory tower was capable of solving the water crisis, they would have done it by now. No one else is offering a solution like this – certainly not researchers."

I raised my eyebrows. "That's what research is: looking for solutions. We've made a lot of strides."

"Maybe you have, but I think you'll find that there are a lot more innovators amongst CEOs than PhDs," he said. "This is not my first rodeo."

"Though it is your first pipeline," I countered.

He let out a laugh, easy and light.

How could he be so casual, so cavalier? I could hear my heart beating in my ears, and my breath was so heavy I had to make sure I didn't have my mouth open.

"I run a hedge fund managing fifty-six billion in assets, Suzy." He winked. "I think I can handle one water pipe."

This was where I should have taken Carl's advice. I should have stopped, thought about what was about to come out of my mouth, and made the decision to shut up.

But I cannot shut up.

"You know what they say," I said evenly, reflecting his stupid smile right back at him. "There's no situation a hedge fund can't make worse, and no industry you or your buddies in private equity can't run into the ground for the greater good of your wallets."

Dolly laughed. "A lively debate if I ever saw one. Thank you both, that's all the time we have for now. I'm Dolly Figs, and this is Issues at Eleven."

CHAPTER FOUR

Leo

There is no force on earth like the intuition of a worried mother. My mom, despite being nearly a thousand miles away, somehow sensed I'd made the proposal and called me the next day.

"I don't know, Leo," she said, her voice low. "Are you sure this is a good idea?"

"Why are you whispering?" I tucked the phone under my ear and squatted down. There was one box left to unpack, and I wanted it done before Anna arrived. "Don't worry. It's going to be fine."

The university had given me far more space than I needed – an office, a separate studio, and a private storage space. One wall of the office was all windows, and another was entirely bookshelves. This last box of books would just barely fit.

"What kind of woman would accept so much money from someone she doesn't even know?"

"She hasn't accepted yet."

A huff rang out from the other side of the phone. "Does she think she's too good for my Leo?"

"No, it's not like that, she's—"

"Because I told you I have a friend, and her niece could do it. No problem. No questions."

I unloaded the books and broke down the box before tossing it into the pile. "I'm not going to pretend to be engaged to a twenty-two-year-old, Mama. That's ten years younger than me."

She harrumphed. "This woman, how old is she?"

"I don't know. Closer to my age." Definitely not a dewy-eyed youth. I'd met enough of those in New York: fresh from art school, fully confident that love and fame were just around the corner – and, more often than not, that both of these desires would be fulfilled by me.

"She has no husband?" A pause. "There must be something wrong with her."

I let out a laugh. "I don't think so, Mama."

"All those beautiful girls chasing after you, and you go for a lonely old maid?"

There was a knock at the office door. "Mama, I have to go. I think she's here. Try not to worry, okay?"

"I always worry." A sigh. "Good luck."

There was nothing to worry about.

Probably.

I ended the call and yelled, "Come in!" before realizing in that second I'd left the pile of flattened boxes on the floor. I grabbed them, stuffing them inside the closet as Anna walked in.

The scent of fresh outdoor air lingered on her coat. She looked different today – cooler, in a way. I wondered if it was intentional. Her hair was pulled into a ponytail and she had sunglasses on top of her head, her expression calm and unaffected.

Maybe she didn't need the money as badly as I thought. Maybe I had miscalculated this whole thing and my mom was right...

"Nice office you've got here," she said, her eyes scanning the windows, the desk, and the now-filled shelves. "Was it part of the lure to get you to teach here?"

I smiled. "What makes you think they had to lure me?"

"I looked you up." She ran a hand over one of the white leather chairs the art department had insisted on giving me. "Can I sit?"

"Please do. Would you like some coffee? Tea?"

She took off her coat and shook her head. "I'm here to talk business."

Well.

She went on. "I'm not going to pretend to know anything about art, but the internet tells me you're kind of a big deal."

Anna took a seat, her expression flat and unreadable.

At least she was engaging with me. That was a good sign. I followed her lead and took a seat behind the desk. "I don't know if that's true, but I've had some success, yes."

"It seems like you lived the artist's life in New York City. A partier's life."

I picked up my coffee mug and held it in both hands. It was already cold because I'd gotten carried away with unpacking. "That's all behind me now."

She leaned in ever so slightly. "Why?"

"Too old for it." I took a sip, then set the mug down. "What else did you find out about me?"

"Nothing, really." Anna crossed her arms and sat back. "I was hoping I'd find out more about this man I'm supposedly going to marry."

So she was interested. Cautious, but interested. "Feel free to ask whatever you like."

She kept her eyes fixed on me, her head slightly tilted. For a moment she was quiet, and I thought I'd have to try to come up with something to sell myself, but the silence was short-lived.

"Why do you need me to be your fiancée?"

The one thing she wanted to know was the one thing I wasn't ready to tell her. "It's nothing nefarious."

"Lying about an engagement is kind of nefarious."

"You're right." I stopped to gather my thoughts. "What I can tell you is that I need to impress someone."

She frowned. "Is it for an inheritance?"

"No." I had plenty of money. If she'd searched my name, she probably knew that. "It's nothing like that."

"Do you need a green card?"

I shook my head. "No."

She sat back, tapping a finger on the armrest. "I don't get it. What's the catch?"

"There's no catch." I clasped my hands and rested my arms on the desk. "People just need to believe it's real. We'll need to come up with a convincing backstory and make it look like this is a legitimate engagement."

"Ah. You need a hundred-thousand-dollar performance?"

That was one way to put it. I nodded. "It will take a few months, and you'll have to spend time with me. Even your own friends and family have to believe it's real."

She let out a laugh. "My family? Why?"

"If anyone suspects this is fake, everything will fall apart."

"And I don't get paid."

That seemed harsh, but since we were talking business... "Yes."

She narrowed her eyes. "Why can't you tell me what this is about?"

I took a deep breath. "Because I don't trust you yet."

Her eyebrows flashed up. "Okay. Fine. Why don't you hire an actress, then?"

"I need someone serious. Someone who won't..." How to put this without sounding vain? "Get emotional. Or attached."

There was a slight flicker at the corner of her mouth. "So your criteria is a serious person who speaks Polish and won't fall in love with you." She uncrossed her arms. "You need me to impress some Polish snob?"

"In a way, yes. We'll have to make a trip to Poland. It could last a week, maybe more."

She nodded. "A hundred thousand to convince everyone we're madly in love, plus a trip to Poland?"

I nodded.

Anna tucked a strand of hair behind her ear, momentarily stopping her interrogation.

I took the opportunity to speak. "I'll pay you half of the money now, and the other half after a successful trip."

She let out a sigh. "What does successful mean? That's too subjective."

Of course. I had to remember I was dealing with an engineer. She wanted facts, numbers, dates. "It'll be obvious. Not subjective."

"You should know my uncle owns a meat market. If anything happens to me..." She took her hand and dragged a finger across her neck. "They *will* blame you."

I suppressed a smile. "Understood."

A silence fell between us, and I made the decision not to break it. I had told her all I could for the time being, and I didn't want to waste my time convincing her.

I needed someone who would be as invested in this as I was. Considering the GoFundMe she'd started for her brother's legal fees was still hovering at eight hundred dollars, Anna was a star candidate.

As a bonus, if I had to spend a lot of time with someone over the next few months, it might as well be someone interesting to talk to and pleasant to look at.

Anna stood, darting a hand into her purse. For a second I had the mad thought she was going to pull a knife on me, but instead, she secured the purse strap on her shoulder and leaned forward, hand outstretched.

"Then we have a deal."

I stood, grasping her small, cool palm in my hand. "Great."

"When should we get started on this story of ours?"

"As soon as possible."

Anna puffed out her cheeks and nodded. "Okay, I have some ideas. We can—" She paused, peering through the window behind me. "Did you know there's a helipad out there?"

I'd heard the commotion of a helicopter coming down, but I hadn't thought anything of it. Life here was still much quieter than what I was used to. I turned to see the blades of a black helicopter slowing to a halt. "Huh. Guess this office isn't so peaceful after all."

"I've *never* seen a helicopter land here." She stood, going to the window. "There's a guy hopping out."

I squinted. "Is that Ken Fielding?"

She let out a groan. "Do you know him?"

"No. I mean, he's a famous billionaire. He started that company that's making ecofriendly planes."

Her face scrunched, settling into a scowl. "That's weird."

"I can't believe you don't know who he is." I watched as Ken disappeared into one of the university buildings.

"We just became acquainted." She turned away from the window and took a seat. "I think I know why he's here."

"Probably to poach the top engineers from your department."

"No. To get me fired after I insulted him on the local news." Anna pulled her phone out of her pocket and stared at it, her expression flat again. "Oh good, my boss is calling me. I'm sure this isn't related to Ken Fielding showing up."

I stared at her, forgetting myself for the first time in months. She was riveting. I had no idea what was going to come out of her mouth next. "Aren't you going to answer?"

"Do I have to?" She peered up at me. "Are you going to be one of those controlling fiancés? I don't think I can handle that."

I put my hands up. "No. Do whatever you need to do."

"He's calling again," she muttered, seemingly more to herself than to me. "I'll answer, but I'm not happy about it."

I had to turn my head to hide my laughter. This was going to be an interesting few months.

CHAPTER FIVE

Anna

I t's never pleasant when the consequences of your actions chase after you, insistent on slapping you in the face, even when you've rather heroically tried to outrun them.

I had no one to blame but myself. And maybe Carl.

I cleared my throat, intent on heading off a scolding. "Hi, Carl. Before you yell at me, remember that *you* made me go on that show. You are nearly sixty-seven years old and should know better."

"Anna, I've been looking for you!"

He was chipper, and who was I kidding? Carl never scolded me, even when I deserved it. "Oh really?"

"You've got a visitor. Ken just stopped by. Ken Fielding. You remember him?"

I shut my eyes. "Yes."

"He enjoyed your conversation and is interested in potentially working with you – and with us."

Great. An offer I couldn't refuse because I wasn't allowed to, not for queen, country, and career. "I'm in the art building right now, but—"

"We'll head over. Where can we meet you?"

I begrudgingly told him Leo's office number, then hung up, staring out the window.

"Everything all right?" Leo asked, leaning back against a bookshelf, arms crossed over his chest.

"No." I slumped forward, resting my face in my hands.

"Were you fired?"

"Worse." I let out a groan and sat up. "I think I'm going to have to be nice to Ken Fielding."

He shrugged. "That doesn't seem so bad."

Easy for him to say, with his muscular arms and his windowed office with books to the ceiling and fancy chairs and a desk that didn't predate the fall of the Berlin Wall.

Leo didn't have to answer to anyone, whereas I had to agree to every committee, every teaching "opportunity," and every collaboration just to have a shot at a tenure-track position.

For once, I managed to hold my tongue. The fact that the ten thousand dollars burning a hole in my purse was *mine*, and I could take it to the courthouse and bail my brother out *today* was enough to keep me quiet.

"You're right," I replied. I meant it, in a way.

I got up, intent on finding a book to pretend to read, but they arrived too quickly. Within moments, there was a knock, and Leo opened the door.

"Hi. Welcome." He waved a hand, and in walked Carl, followed closely by Ken.

Ken was taller than I'd imagined after seeing him on that little screen. He was different today, too, dressed more casually in a fitted athletic t-shirt, his chest and arms firm and toned under the shining fabric.

Billionaire body, I guess. He probably only ate lean foods, grown in hydro chambers on his property and prepared by his team of personal chefs.

The t-shirt was a nice touch, nearly making him look like an Everyman.

"Nice to see you again, Anna," he said, with a smile and a shallow bow of his head.

"Hi Ken."

"I was busy boring Ken," Carl said in his soft voice, "telling him about the man the engineering building was named after."

Carl was genuinely happy just to be here. The man could've retired twenty years ago, but he loved his job too much. He loved the scholarly conversations, sitting in a room and hashing out ideas, debating the merits of deep learning with hydrologic models for turbulent heat fluxes.

It was adorable in a way, but as I liked to remind him, by not retiring he was keeping the position from opening up for someone like, say, me.

Carl never took offense to these comments telling him to quit his job. He'd laugh and nod his head. "You're not wrong, Anna, but you could learn to soften your rightness."

I had a feeling this was going to be another teachable moment for Carl.

"I wasn't bored at all," Ken said. "It's fascinating how we all came to be where we are, isn't it?"

I almost said *not really* but Leo interjected, "Hi, nice to meet you both. I'm Leo," which was probably for the best.

"He's just signed on to teach here," I added.

Carl turned to him and shook his hand. "Welcome to Madison."

Leo nodded. "Thanks."

Ken looked back at me. "You're obviously busy and I don't want to take up any more of your time, so I'll be brief."

At least it would be over soon. I forced myself to smile.

"Next week I'll be in Zermatt for the Universal Venture Roundtable."

He paused, as if waiting for me to exclaim in excitement.

I did not do this.

Carl took the opportunity to educate us. "It was founded by an engineer, you know."

"No way. Really?" Ken turned toward him, mouth slightly open. "It makes perfect sense. We still think like engineers. We meet every year, trying to find unique solutions to complicated problems. I'm sure you've heard of it."

He looked tentatively at me, but I shook my head. "I don't think I have."

I was lying, of course. I'm not an idiot, but sometimes—and I think I get this from my grandfather, the ultimate instigator—I can't help myself.

Ken was unfazed. "It's a meeting of world leaders, innovators, investors – everyone who's anyone, really. We come together to improve the world."

To improve the world! What terribly important geniuses they all must be.

I knew my role was to play the impressed damsel, but I couldn't do it. "Oh. Wow."

He hesitated, scanning my face before speaking again. "I know we didn't get off on the best foot, but I'd like to change that. I think you need to be at the meeting. You're obviously brilliant, and frankly, the organization would benefit from your discerning mind."

Carl clasped his hands together. "How wonderful, Anna! What an opportunity! No one from Madison has ever been invited to Zermatt."

There it was. I was going to be held professionally hostage by this blowhard.

Unless... What if it was worse than that? What if it wasn't just professional? Was Mr. Tight Shirt Ken hitting on me?

I glanced at Leo, my supposed fiancé, but he didn't return my gaze. He had the slightest smile on the edge of his lips.

So smug over there. I bet he didn't have to tiptoe around romantic advances to ensure his career wasn't beaten down like an out-of-control soufflé.

I had to answer, so I forced myself to say, "That sounds amazing."

A smile spread across Ken's face, revealing his dazzlingly white smile. "Wonderful."

I couldn't bear it. I couldn't take standing there, having to do this stupid trip after I went on that stupid news show.

I should have shut up, but, as always, I could not shut up.

"I have one question," I added.

Ken grinned. "Anything."

"Can my fiancé come?"

CHAPTER SIX

Leo

After Ken graciously extended the Zermatt invitation to me, he made a quick exit, the excitement disappearing as hastily as it appeared.

I'd met a fair number of Kens in recent years, or what my agent referred to as The Ruling Class. Artists tended to fall into two camps when it came to their masters: those who were happy to become pets, falling over themselves to please, and those who overflowed with disdain.

It didn't much make a difference; we cashed the checks all the same.

Oddly, it didn't seem like Anna realized how remarkable it was that a man like Ken Fielding had flown to Wisconsin to see her. There was a chance his interest was purely professional, but it seemed unlikely. The look he'd given me after Anna introduced me as her fiancé suggested he was sizing me up, deciding how quickly Anna would dump me to take a spot on his arm.

Judging from the mere seconds he spent looking at me, he didn't think it would take long.

Anna was free to do whatever she wanted once our deal was done. The only edge I had over Ken was that I was offering the money now, immediately, when she needed it.

Still. I didn't want to draw attention to the fact that my hundred-thousand-dollar offer was nothing compared to what Ken had, so I decided not to say anything about my suspicions.

As soon as the door closed, however, Anna announced, "Am I crazy, or was Ken hitting on me?"

So much for keeping it to myself. "Seems like it."

She narrowed her eyes, a smile tugging at her mouth. "Aren't you jealous?"

I shook my head. "That's not my style."

"Great. My fiancé doesn't even care that another man is trying to whisk me away to Sweden."

"Switzerland," I corrected, "and if you think this will get me to increase your fee, you're wrong."

Anna let out a laugh, dropping into a chair. "No. He's gross."

Her disgust seemed genuine. I knew which category of artist she'd fall into, and she clearly didn't have to be nice to people like Ken. The university provided all she needed, and she could live on the validity of her work alone.

That was the life I could live, too, if I could only adjust. No more catering to The Ruling Class, laughing at their jokes, listening to them drone on about their art opinions.

"Sorry I brought you into it," she added. "You don't have to go. I just needed him to know I was taken."

"There's no way I'm missing it," I said, taking a seat behind my desk. "I'll never get an invitation again, and tickets are over a hundred thousand dollars apiece."

Her eyes bulged. "What? I hope he doesn't expect me to pay for myself."

"I'm sure he doesn't, which makes it even funnier that you invited me."

She smiled, then laughed, then progressed to what could only be described as a cackle. Once that passed, she said, "Good. Let him pay for it."

"Now that you've outed us, we should figure out our backstory."

The smile disappeared from her face and she let out a heavy breath. "You're right. Poor Carl looked so shocked when I said you were my fiancé. He's always so interested in my life."

"He's your boss?"

"Yeah. Great guy. I'll have to tell him you're an old friend or something. How long were you living in New York City?"

"About twenty years."

"Okay, I'll say I met you when I was at Columbia, and we've been writing to each other ever since. That's perfect. We reconnected and decided to get married."

"You were the one that got away," I offered.

Anna squinted, moving her head in a slow nod. "Yes, that's cute. No one will question that."

"Won't your friends think it's odd you never mentioned me?"

"None of my friends went to Columbia," she said with the wave of a hand. "They only knew my life from afar. I can sell it."

"And your family?"

She let out a sigh. "I don't see why they have to be involved."

Because somehow all Polish people seemed to know each other. "Because that's the deal."

Anna stared at me. I could see the wheels turning in her head, and I stayed silent.

"They're not going to be nice to you," she finally said.

"I don't need them to be nice to me."

Her eyes darted to me before looking away, down at her hands, then out through the window. "There are some things you should probably know about me."

We were getting down to details. Good. Other than attracting that billionaire, she was doing everything I'd hoped she'd do. Taking this seriously, making a plan.

I pulled a journal out of my desk drawer. "I'm going to take notes."

"Smart."

She took a deep breath and began. She was born in Chicago, the eldest of four. Her mom ran a cleaning business, her dad was an elevator mechanic. They left Poland in the eighties, ended up in Madison after a few years, and sought the best school districts.

It paid off. Anna got a full ride to Columbia for engineering. The second born, Sarah, was a nurse, married with two kids in Chicago. The third, Lisa, was an attorney. She hated it, but made "piles of money," per Anna.

"What's with the names?" I asked.

Anna frowned. "What do you mean?"

"Why are your siblings' names so American?"

"Oh." She laughed. "First of all, my parents love America. Second of all, they named us after movies they liked. Sarah from *Terminator*. Lisa from *Coming to America*. My brother Frankie – Frank Cross in *Scrooged*."

"And you?"

"Suzanna Hamilton, the lead actress in the 1984 adaptation of Orwell's *Nineteen Eighty-four*. It's one of my dad's favorite books."

"Ah."

"I think they got confused," she continued, "because Zuzanna is Polish, and they saw Suzanna and thought it was a common American name. They call me Zuzia. You should know that. Write that down."

I wrote *Zuzia* at the top of the sheet.

"We're Polish, so no one's name is actually their name. We all have, like, seven nicknames."

"I get that," I said. "Russians do the same thing. My dad calls me Leva."

She blinked at me. "What?"

"My dad," I said, clearing my throat. "He calls me Leva."

"Why?"

"Same reason, I guess?"

"But he's not Russian."

I looked up from my notes. They'd already filled two pages. "He is."

"You said your mom was Polish."

"Yeah, and my dad's Russian."

Her voice dropped to nearly a whisper. "You didn't mention that."

"What does it matter? I was born in Russia. My parents were granted asylum after fleeing."

Anna stood up, then sat, then stood up again. She covered her mouth with her hand and stared at me.

"What?" I asked. "Do you need some paper?"

"This isn't going to work."

I dropped the journal onto my desk. "What's not going to work?"

"You're *Russian?* Do you have any idea how Poles feel about *Russians?*"

I did, which was why I needed her. My father's homeland was not popular wherever I went, but especially in Poland. "My mom is Polish."

"Doesn't matter," she said, shaking her head. "My mom will just say she's an idiot for marrying your father."

"My dad was in prison for four years for speaking out against the government."

She grimaced. "Doesn't matter."

I stood from my desk and took a seat next to her. "Your parents are free to hate me. That's fine. I can take it."

"It's going to be a tough sell," she said, scratching the back of her neck.

"At least I know what to expect." I leaned forward, resting my elbows on my knees. "I appreciate your honesty, but my father is a renowned Russian mathematics professor. I can't possibly disappoint your parents more than I've disappointed him."

She raised her eyebrows.

I went on. "I only get one shot to get this engagement right. I think we can do it, but if you don't—"

"No." She straightened her shoulders and sat back. "It'll work. I'm just – I felt like you deserved to be warned."

"When can I meet your family? Before we go to Zermatt?"

She stared down at the floor. "That would be this weekend."

"This weekend, then." I stood. "That gives me time to study your family history."

"Study. Yeah. It'll be fine." Anna nodded. "It'll be fine."

CHAPTER SEVEN

Anna

It most certainly was not going to be fine, but what was I supposed to do, admit that to Leo? Lose ten thousand dollars and let my baby brother rot in a cell? He'd probably have to join a gang for protection, then my mom would threaten the gang leader and get hauled into jail herself, only to create her own gang and start the process over again.

Plus, I'd found *the* best criminal defense attorney in Wisconsin, and he'd agreed to take Frankie's case. I didn't know his full fee yet, but to cover everything start to finish would be at least eighty thousand dollars.

My family, bless their industrious hearts, wouldn't be able to come up with the money in time. Even pulling together with my generous aunts, uncles, and cousins wouldn't cut it, and not because my mom wouldn't let Frankie accept the money. It was also because no one in the family knew about Frankie's troubles.

Officially, at least. Everything is a secret to my family. The CIA has nothing on them. It starts with an aunt saying, "Promise you won't tell anyone, but..." followed by something like, "Frankie got arrested again," or "Jacek has diabetes," or

"Karolina got in a fight with her hairdresser and ended up with half a haircut."

(That one was pretty funny. She doesn't trust anyone else with her hair, so after the fight, she walked around with the back of her hair four inches shorter than the sides until they made up.)

This process repeats, crossing the Atlantic a hundred times until my entire extended family has taken a vow to tell no one, while simultaneously informing everyone they come across – the butcher, their Uber driver, the lady leaving dog poo on their front lawn – about the "secret."

Not that it mattered. Frankie's not-so-secret arrest was going to be old news when I busted onto the scene with a Russian fiancé.

You'd think getting arrested for a felony would be more scandalous than getting engaged, but no. Crimes could be explained, innocence professed.

Marriage was for life, and marriage to a Russian?

Unthinkable.

I am not exaggerating (as I am admittedly prone to do). To understand why my family—my mother in particular—despises Russians *so* much, you have to go back. Way, way back, to World War II.

We have to go that far because while the Polish people are known for many things – delicious food, Pope John Paul II, and world-class complaining – there is perhaps nothing they are better known for than their stubbornness.

Poland was literally wiped from the map for over a hundred years, folded into this country or that empire, yet they managed to claw their way back. These people are *stubborn*, and they can hold a grudge.

The most recent assault started with the Nazi invasion. You'll recall Hitler invaded Poland from the west and Stalin invaded from the east. When the Nazis turned on their allies, however, the Soviets switched sides, landing Stalin a seat at the winner's table. When he got there, his top priority was Poland.

Yes, Poland! Little old Poland!

How we've sinned against these Poles, he cried, taking it upon himself to give Poland the gift of a Soviet-backed government. That way, he reasoned, Russia was protected from further invasion, and Poland could flourish under his warm communist gaze.

Poland was not happy about this, so the new government undertook the task of trying to Soviet-ize the Poles. They attacked the beloved Catholic church, forced the Poles to learn Russian in school, and sent them to Siberia for crimes, real and imagined – you know, everything that could enrage the people of Poland the most.

To make a long story of stubbornness short, the Soviets failed. Miserably. The Poles rose up again and again, finally getting their country back and inspiring other Soviet Bloc countries to shake their iron chains.

This freedom didn't happen, however, before my parents left Poland. They left the ration cards, the bread lines, and the comfort of being near their families. They left the comfort of the only world they'd ever known, but the one thing they did *not* leave behind was their grudge against Russia.

They held onto that tightly, my mom in particular. I've tried to tell her that her fight is with the Russian *government* and not the Russian *people*. I've insisted there is no one the Russian government is crueler to than their own people, but she won't hear it. To her, when the Devil himself steps out of hell, he will be speaking Russian.

This made my new engagement more than awkward. It was a disaster, but I had no choice but to call her and have the most difficult conversation of my life.

I waited until I was in the car, hoping to keep it short and sandwiched with good news.

"Mama?" I said innocently, "I'm on my way to bail Frankie out."

"You have the money?" she gasped. "How did you do it?"

"I had help from an old friend."

"Frankie is coming home!" she yelled, and I could hear the low rumbles of my dad's voice as he got near the phone. "Hang on," she said, "I am going to put you on speaker."

Their voices echoed, distorted and completely unintelligible.

"I can't hear either of you. Did you cover the microphone?"

Rustling, then, "Can you hear me now?"

"Yes, I can hear you." I cleared my throat. Mix the bad news in with good news. That was the way to do it. "I'm going to pick him up, but I wanted to talk to you."

"We have to make a party," she said. "Saturday. Maybe Lisa can come? Sarah is probably busy. I think she's working."

"Yeah, yeah." My heart was thundering in my ears, but there was no way around it. They had to know. "Mama, listen. I'm going to bring someone this weekend."

"Carl? I like Carl! Last time he forgot his wine opener, we can—"

"Not Carl. Someone else." I cleared my throat. "You know how I've been lonely recently."

"What do you have to feel lonely about? You don't need anyone."

My dad's voice chimed in. "If you're feeling lonely, you can do what I do. Order two meals, pretend one is for your boyfriend, then eat them both."

I smiled. "Tata, since when do you pretend you have a boyfriend?"

"Whenever I'm really hungry."

I heard the distinct sound of my mom smacking him. "Zuzia, you can come over if you're lonely. Why don't you come over more?"

I should've known they were going to make it nearly impossible for me to have a serious conversation.

I let out a sigh and steadied my voice. "I've decided to make a change. I'm thirty years old. I'm an adult—"

My mom's laugh burst through. "Oh yes, you're a big adult. We know."

I shut my eyes. "An old friend helped me with Frankie's bail and – listen, we always said if we weren't married by thirty, that we'd get married. So we're getting married."

"Zuzia, that's not funny. What should I make for Saturday?"

"I'm not joking. His name is Leo. He's a professor."

"A professor," my mom cooed, the laughter still in her voice.

"Professor of Love," my dad quipped.

Stay on course. "He's an art professor."

My mom didn't miss a beat. "So he teaches the arts and crafts majors?"

"Fine arts," I corrected. "I'm going to bring him on Saturday."

The sound of pots and pans clinked in the background. "Tell Frankie we'll have szarlotka for dessert!"

I hated to ruin her joy. Technically, I'd told her. That was enough for now. "I'm almost there. I'll let him know."

. . .

The jail was in its usual state, with drab, peeling walls, bored employees, and endless locking gates and buzzers. I'd been visiting Frankie three times a week, but shockingly, the place never grew on me.

After two hours of waiting, Frankie emerged, dressed in a black hoodie and jeans. His face was thinner than when he'd gone in, and there were light purple bags under his eyes, but he still had his adorable half-smile and dimples.

He gave a little wave as he walked toward me. "Hey."

"I'm glad they didn't shave your curls." I hugged him and scrubbed his head with my hand.

Frankie pulled away, grinning. "No, they didn't mess with my hair."

"Are you okay?"

He nodded, looking down, and his smile fell. "I'm okay."

My heart pinched in my chest, and I had to look away from him so I wouldn't burst into tears. That wasn't what he needed right now. "I found the *best* lawyer for you. We're going to meet with him in two weeks and talk about your case."

"I was going to meet with the guy Brandon and Jamie are using."

The dud lawyer his two idiot friends found? No way. Not for my brother. "Brandon and Jamie are morons. Trust me. This guy is amazing."

We walked through the doors of the jail and into the fresh fall air. There was a warm glow from the streetlamps and crinkly leaves under our feet.

Life was good again. It had to be.

Frankie peered over at me. "Mama said you got the money from a balloon artist or something?"

Balloon artist. She had heard me after all. Sort of.

I shook my head. "He's an art professor."

Frankie chuckled. "*Oh.*"

"How did she already talk to you? I just got off the phone with her a few hours ago."

"She called and told the warden it was an emergency, that we had to talk, and then she asked me if I was okay with one dessert or if I wanted two." He laughed, shaking his head.

"Ah. Well, I told her I'm getting married." It was good to hear him laugh. We got to my car and I unlocked the doors. "She didn't seem like she believed me."

"They believe you, kind of. They think you made it up. You don't want to know what Tata said."

"I'm sure I'll hear it tomorrow." I opened my door and slid into the seat. "Mama is hosting a welcome home dinner for you."

He got into the car and closed his eyes. "I told her one dessert was fine, but she decided to make two anyway."

"Do you want to sleep at their house tonight?" Despite having an apartment of his own, my brother often popped home for the food, the hospitality, and, let's be honest, the overflowing love.

"Nah. I'm tired. I think I'll go to sleep."

"I'll take you home."

I pulled out of my parking spot, the radio playing a soft Andrew Bird song, his whistling filling in the background.

I glanced at Frankie before turning onto the street. He had his eyes closed and looked half asleep. I turned the music down.

Close to his apartment, I tried to take a speed bump as gently as possible, but it roused him.

"Zuzia?"

I looked over at him. His eyes were opened, just a sliver. "Yeah?"

"Thanks for coming to get me."

I turned away, pinching my lips and trying to squeeze the tears back in. "Anytime, Frankie."

CHAPTER EIGHT

Leo

My phone wouldn't stop ringing. I was trying to unpack a few boxes and make my house look presentable, but the phone would not stop.

It was my agent. I hadn't produced anything in months, so there was nothing for him to sell, nothing for him to hype. It left him with far too much time to bother me.

I tried reminding myself there was once a time I appreciated him. Needed him, really. I was a young artist then, desperate for validation, for someone to tell me my work was worthwhile, that I hadn't wasted my life swimming in oils. A psychologist might say I was desperate to prove my father wrong; they might be right. I don't know.

That life was behind me now. The parties, the competitors disguised as friends, the life of doing things without knowing why I was doing them. It felt like it had never been my life, never been *me,* as though it had all happened to someone else.

The only part that was mine was the call ending it. That was the only part I could still feel – the bile rising in my throat, the hole opening in my chest.

It was my dad who had made the call. I can only assume because my mother was unable to speak, but I'll never know because I'll never ask.

"Leo," he said simply, "your brother is gone."

That evening I had been in the same place I always was, at a party I didn't want to attend, and I had to duck outside to hear him. My ears were still ringing from the music. "Gone? Gone where?"

"He's dead, Leo. Dima is dead."

And that was the end of my life in New York City.

I opened a box with pictures and pulled out one of me and my brother. He was young then, twenty. Just a kid, really, but even now he looked older than I felt. Life had not been easy for him.

My phone rang. I shut my eyes.

My agent, again. I had to answer. "Hey."

"Leo! I've been trying to reach you all week." He let out a tsk. "No calls, no emails, no texts? Don't you have service out on that farm?"

I only had a few minutes before Anna would arrive, and I didn't have time to explain, again, that Wisconsin was not one giant farm. "I've been busy."

"Busy, always busy. Making some new paintings, I hope?"

"No, sorry. There's nothing new." I hadn't painted anything since Dima died. I didn't see the point. Maybe there never had been a point.

"Don't start again that you're going to stop painting, Leo! Your star is just beginning to rise. What is with you artists, always destroying everything of beauty, it's like—"

I cut him off. "Yeah, I know. It's like we're all idiots."

He scoffed. "As if telling you what a fool you're being has any effect."

He wasn't wrong. "I'm sorry, man, but I have to go."

"No, wait." He sighed. "I've secured a buyer for your last three paintings. Are you *sure* you want to sell?"

"I am. Clear out the warehouse."

"You know we could drum up a lot more hype if we had a show saying these are your final pieces."

I didn't know how to tell him I didn't care without sounding cruel, so I said, "Whatever you think is best."

A car sputtered into the driveway. I peeked through the window and saw an old, grandma-blue Honda minivan.

Not what I expected Anna to be driving. Had she brought an entire soccer team? Why did she need a van?

She looked up, and I ducked away from the window. I really needed to get blinds. And curtains. Furniture would be nice, too.

"Leo?"

"I have to go. Sell them." I paused. That was harsh. I didn't mean to sound like that. I softened my voice. "I'm sorry. Thank you again. I mean it."

Another sigh. "I'll be here when you need me."

I ended the call and grabbed my coat. It would be better to meet Anna outside. My house was still a work in progress, and I wasn't ready for her questions.

When I opened the front door, she was only a few steps away, fighting against the wind whipping hair across her face and tearing at her dress.

As absurd as this situation was, my first thought was how nice she looked. She wore a blue dress with pink flowers, with a jean jacket she was tugging closed across her chest in a vain attempt to block the wind.

Was this what meeting the parents was like? It was a sort of sweet moment, wholesome in a way. None of my previous girlfriends had brought me to meet their parents.

There might be something to that.

"You ever heard of a lawn mower?" she yelled, releasing her jacket to sweep an arm over the lawn.

The lawn – my lawn, I guess – was tall and wispy as beachgrass, dancing elegantly in the wind. "I don't have one yet."

"You'd better ask the neighbors to borrow one, or someone will report you to the HOA."

"I'm in an HOA?"

Her hands dropped to her sides. "Yeah. Dude, do you even live here?"

"I've never lived in a house before. Just apartments." I actually preferred the grass this way. It looked wild and free, like it hadn't yet been cut down by life, like it had some hope for its future. I liked that quality in grass.

"Okay, Mr. Manhattan." She stared at me, hands on her hips. "In the suburbs, there are certain things you must do to avoid the wrath of your neighbors. Cut the grass, don't host loud parties, wear pants when you go outside."

I looked down. "Two out of three isn't bad."

She looked past me, scanning the house with her keen stare. "This is a nice house in a good school district. How did you manage to find it?"

I wasn't sure what she meant. Buying a house was far easier than finding a place to rent in New York City.

It wasn't perfect. I didn't go for perfect. In truth, it was bigger than I needed: a four bedroom, three bath palace.

The yard was what sold me, though. I could envision blooms in the spring, and bubbles floating over the wooden deck, popping and leaving a film where they landed. In the heat of the summer, there would be a blow-up pool, a dog fetching sticks and digging holes. It'd be a nice place to paint, if I were still doing that.

"I made a cash offer," I said with a shrug.

"You seem to make a lot of those." She flashed a smile and a laugh burst out of me.

When I'd come up with this scheme, this idea of hiring a fiancée, I didn't have much time to think. I just acted.

It could have all gone horribly wrong, but I found *her*. If anyone could pull it off, it was Anna. It seemed like she could do anything.

"We should go," she said, "I told my mom we'd be there at one."

"Right." I took a few steps, an odd feeling of emptiness drifting in. I'd forgotten something. "Hang on a second."

I jogged back to the house and grabbed the bouquet I'd gotten for Anna's mom. Anna stared as I ran back, her gaze fixed on the flowers.

"Do you like them?" I asked, holding up the bouquet.

She nodded, pulling open the driver's side door. "We should go."

I followed her to the car and got into the passenger seat. "What's with the minivan?"

She cast me a hurried glance as she buckled her seatbelt. "What do you mean?"

"Do you have four kids I don't know about?"

She shot me a look. "No kids. My uncle gave me a good price on it. What, is it not cool enough for you?"

I turned, hiding my smile by looking out the window. "No, very cool."

"Your SUV looks pretty nice. You could drive us in that."

"Eh... still getting used to being on the road."

"I can't believe my fiancé is a bad driver." She shook her head. "Listen, I told my parents about you. About *us*. I said we'd made a pact that if we weren't married by thirty, we'd marry each other."

"Oh. Smart." I paused. That was exactly the excuse I'd come up with. Either we thought alike, or we were both simple. Maybe both. "How'd they take the news?"

"About as expected." She bit her lip, still staring straight ahead. "My mom started referring to you as a balloon artist."

I smiled. "She and my dad would get along."

"No," she said firmly. "They would not."

She gripped the steering wheel like it owed her money.

Speaking of. "I wired the first half of the payment to the account you gave me."

"Oh. Thanks."

An abrupt silence took hold. Anna was awkward about money. Or maybe she was being awkward because of her reason for needing it?

At least, what I assumed was the reason. I had to guess and search online, because unlike a real fiancé, I didn't know about her life.

It wasn't hard to guess, though. Her brother Frankie was in a tenuous situation.

Allegedly, he and his two friends had stolen an RV camper and taken it for a joy ride. That was bad enough – grand theft of a motor vehicle – but it got worse. There was a couple asleep in the back of the RV, which added two charges of kidnapping.

It all seemed silly to me, but with those charges, Frankie could spend the rest of his life in prison.

I looked over at her. She was still focused on the road. I'd yet to find a way to bring up Frankie's situation without seeming crass.

Anna caught my glance and cleared her throat. "I was thinking. Do we need to, I don't know, be affectionate or anything?"

That was a good question. "Are you normally affectionate with your boyfriends?"

"I don't have boyfriends."

I laughed. She did not.

"You've never had a boyfriend?" I asked.

"I've had boyfriends, just not ones I brought home." She flinched. "Except one time. It was a mistake."

"Yeah?"

She shook her head, her gaze focused on the road.

After more silence, I asked, "Did they ever find his body?"

"Ha. No." She paused. "You have to understand, my mom never wanted me to get married."

"Huh. That's interesting."

"No kids, no husband. That was her motto." Anna shrugged.

"So you hate men and children?"

"What?" She looked at me, her face scrunched. "No. It's just – you can't have a career if you're chasing after a family. 'You can't have it all.' That was her favorite thing to tell me growing up."

"I see."

"So, if she's mean to you..." She sighed. "No, *when* she's mean to you, don't take it personally. It's not the life she wanted for me."

"Got it."

And I did. I'd often wondered what my mom's life would've been like had she not married my father, or married at all. He wasn't a bad person – life is too complicated to designate people as good or bad.

He, too, is complicated. A brilliant mathematician and a staunch supporter of human rights, even at the cost of his own safety, and the safety of his wife and children. I often felt like an afterthought to him, and I'm sure my mom has as well, though she never said it out loud.

Anna slowed the van and turned into the driveway of a small house. The lawn was perfectly trimmed, not a single dandelion in sight. The walkway was lined with flowers and bushes, colorful and bright, and the porch was overflowing with plants and hanging baskets.

Her mom must like flowers. Perhaps I'd done something to soften the blow. She was going to love the bouquet.

Anna shut the car off and took a deep breath. "This is going to be fine."

I nodded, peering through the window. "It is."

"It's going to be fine," she repeated before grabbing her purse and opening the car door.

By the time I got out of my seat, she was halfway to the house. I jogged to catch up and the front door opened as I reached Anna's side.

A woman stared out at us. She looked like Anna's clone a few years into the future. Her hair was a rich chestnut, with golden glints catching in the sunlight. Her bright green eyes were lined with delicate makeup, and there was a wide smile on her face.

Until she saw me. Then the smile slipped, settling into a stiff, open-mouthed scowl. Her eyes narrowed, fixed on the flowers in my hand.

I thrust the bouquet forward. "It's so nice to finally meet you. I'm Leo."

She looked down, her lip curling ever so slightly, as though I was offering a bouquet of elegantly arranged dog poo bags. "Hello."

"Hi, Mama." Anna leaned forward and gave her a cheek kiss. "Sorry we're late."

Her mother turned and said over her shoulder, "Did he have to stop at Walmart for carnations?"

Their likeness wasn't just physical, then.

She spun and disappeared inside.

Anna turned to me. "Yeah, you can just toss those on the porch."

"What? Why?"

"They're funeral flowers." She shook her head. "I shouldn't have let you bring them. My mistake."

"It's my funeral, huh?"

"Don't make jokes." She tugged the bouquet from my hand and threw it to the ground. "She doesn't like jokes."

"Everyone likes jokes."

Anna looked at me, let out a sigh, and walked inside.

I stifled a smile. Her parents didn't have to like me; they only had to believe this was real. And the flowers weren't *that* bad. Had I ever been allowed to meet parents in a real relationship, I probably would have brought even uglier flowers.

I stooped and picked up the bouquet before following her inside.

CHAPTER NINE

Anna

He thought this was *funny*. It wasn't going to be so funny when my mom poisoned his barszcz. Or worse, when she told my dad to do it, and he opted for the comedy by way of Ex-Lax.

(That was no joke. He'd done it before, to his friend who, interestingly, was also an artist. The guy was far less successful than Leo, always broke, always asking my parents for money and a place to stay. They'd let him sleep on the couch for a few nights before he'd get into an argument with my mom, insisting he was right about something, and leave in a huff.)

Maybe this was a joke to Leo, but it wasn't to me. This was my life. *I* was the one lying to my family. *I* was the one who had to play the part perfectly or risk losing the money and my brother spending *sixty* years in prison.

Failure was not an option.

We walked into the house and I took off my shoes, motioning for him to follow. Infuriatingly, he managed to take off his shoes single-handedly, still clutching the awful bouquet with the other hand.

"Drop them," I hissed.

"They're not Walmart flowers," he whispered.

I darted my hand out as he pulled back, the carnations colliding with my arm and sending petals into the air.

"You're hurting them!" he whispered, his mouth open in a mock surprise.

I glared at him. "If you wanted her to like the flowers, you shouldn't have been so cheap."

"I didn't know they were cheap." He stood, straightening his posture and plucking one of the damaged carnations from the bunch. "If I don't bring them now, she'll sense weakness."

"Zuzia!"

I spun around and saw my sister Lisa. "Hey!"

Her eyes were wide, but she was smiling. "You brought a guest!"

"This is Leo. My..." I was going to call him my fiancé, but I couldn't get the words out. Instead I went with, "Leo."

She blinked rapidly, her eyelids fluttering. "Wow, I can't believe this! It's so nice to meet you."

"Nice to meet you, too."

Lisa leaned in for a hug, which Leo graciously accepted, bouquet still clutched in his fist.

I could take the flowers from him, beat him over the head with them, and he still would insist on giving them to my mother.

Artists. So stubborn.

Lisa touched my shoulder. "You look nice."

I reached out and touched a strand of her long, shining hair. "This looks amazing. Did you do something to it?"

She waved a hand. "I got a blowout. I have a thing later."

"A thing?" I smiled. "Like a date?"

"I wish. It's a work thing." She tossed her hair over her shoulder. "Stop trying to distract me. I can't believe you didn't tell me about Leo."

"I know. I'm sorry." At least she didn't seem mad. Luckily, Lisa wasn't one to get mad. My sister Sarah, however, had a temper. I'd have to find a gentle way to break the news to her, if my mom hadn't already.

"He's *so* handsome!" She leaned back, looking at me, then at him.

Leo laughed. "Thank you."

I had to resist rolling my eyes.

"Are these for me?" She put a hand toward the flowers, then laughed. "Just kidding."

"They can be. I don't think your mom wants them."

She shot me a look, her smile faltering for only a moment. "What? I'm sure that's not true."

"Lisa." I lowered my voice. "How bad is it?"

"Hm?" She smiled, then nodded toward the kitchen. "Do you want something to drink?"

Deflection and a fake smile. Not good.

She led the way and Leo followed. It felt like we were making our way into a lion's den. The hallway, cluttered with frame after frame of pictures of us kids, was closing in on me.

I couldn't do this. I didn't even know what I was doing.

"Frankie's coming soon," Lisa said over her shoulder. "He was so tired he slept in until noon. Poor guy."

We reached the kitchen, the white cabinets and counter-tops reflecting the sunlight pouring through the windows.

There was light; it was still daytime. It didn't matter if I *could* do it. I had to do it. For Frankie.

Leo turned to me. "What are you having?"

Lisa picked up her champagne flute. "We have champagne, we have beer, wine—"

"Champagne sounds good to me," he said. "Anna?"

Just then, my mom reappeared, an unopened bottle of champagne in her hands.

"I'll have some, too," I said slowly. "To celebrate."

My mom slammed the bottle onto the counter with a clunk. "Celebrate? What do you have to celebrate?"

My shoulders had worked their way up to my ears. I forced them to relax and cleared my throat. "Frankie getting out of jail, to start."

"Hm." She took a deep breath, staring at me, then started to unwrap the foil around the neck of the bottle. "That is something."

I opened the cupboard and fetched two champagne flutes – crystal, as was the Polish tradition. "Do you want one?"

She struggled against the cork, trying to force it out with both hands. "Fine."

Leo stepped forward and outstretched a hand. "Can I help?"

"No." She didn't look up, as if not looking at him would mean he wasn't there.

I glanced at Lisa. She widened her eyes at me and offered a little smile.

I probably should have texted her to get a read on the mood in the house, but I couldn't bring myself to do it. Probably because I didn't *really* want to know how bad it was.

The door to the basement popped open and my dad appeared, carrying a case of beer. "Hey, you made it!"

He set the beer on the floor and gave me a kiss on the cheek. Then he turned to Leo, his brow furrowed, and crossed his arms.

"I heard you came to steal my daughter."

Leo opened his mouth, then hesitated, and my dad smacked him on the shoulder. "Just kidding. We've been trying to get rid of her for years. She talks so much, she kept scaring the other guys away."

"Hey!" I shot him a look. "I don't talk too much."

Leo offered a handshake and raised his voice. "I'm sorry, you'll have to speak up. I'm partially deaf."

My dad laughed a big, open mouth laugh before taking the cursed flowers out of Leo's hand. "I'm Stanley."

"Leo."

I made a mental note to tell Leo not to confuse my dad with my Uncle Stanley in Poland, my Uncle Stanley in the US, my cousin Stanley, or my nephew, Stan.

And to never encourage my dad's jokes again.

My mom thrust the champagne bottle into my dad's hands. "What are you doing? You're supposed to be helping me. Open this."

He pretended to almost drop the bottle, earning a dirty look from my mom, before securing the cork with both hands. "Okay everyone, cover your eyes!"

It took off with a pop, shot into the ceiling, then ricocheted directly into the top of Lisa's head.

"Ow!" She yelled out, cupping her head with her hand. "Tata!"

"You wanted champagne," he said, stifling a laugh and filling the glasses on the counter. "You have to live with the consequences."

My mom hit him with a dishtowel, which only made him crack up. Lisa recovered the rogue cork from the floor and threw it at him, laughing as it bounced off his shoulder.

He picked up two glasses, handing one to me and one to Leo. "Here, Leo. You're going to need this."

Leo accepted it with a smile. "Thank you."

My dad raised his glass. "To Zuzia, who saved Frankie from prison."

"To Zuzia!" they echoed.

My mom was quiet through this, but she raised her glass.

After taking a sip, she set the glass down and crossed her arms. "Zuzia. The daughter who is getting married without even telling her mother."

I sighed. "I *am* telling you. Look, we're here! And you're being told. Mama, this is Leo. Leo, Mama. See?"

"Oh, you think *this* is how it's supposed to work? You show up with a balloon artist and tell me you're getting married? Where is your balloon ring?"

"Mama," Lisa said gently, "maybe she was afraid to tell you."

"Afraid to tell me!" She put her hands on her hips. "Why would she be afraid to tell me! I'm very nice!"

"Did you notice this champagne has a fruity bloom?" my dad announced, sticking his nose into his glass.

We turned to look at him and he added, "I heard them talk like that about wine on YouTube."

I looked back at my mom. "I told you, I've been feeling lonely, so I decided to make a change."

"I thought you were being dramatic, but then you bring this..." She swooped a hand up and down at Leo without looking at him. "This *artist* into my house!"

I set my glass down. "*I'm* the one being dramatic?"

"You are kind of dramatic," Lisa said under her breath.

"What are you talking about?" I turned to her. "You and Mama are the dramatic ones."

Lisa gasped. "I am the *least* dramatic out of everyone."

"*I* am the least dramatic," my mom said, pointing a finger in the air.

"You're all dramatic," my dad said, leaning back against the counter.

My mom turned on him. "You don't care that your daughter has lost her mind and is going to marry a stranger?"

"He's not a stranger, Mama," I said. "I've known him for years."

"He's a stranger to me!" she said.

My dad shrugged. "He seems like a nice guy."

"Is that all you can say? Oh, he seems like a nice guy. Why don't you give him the keys for the house, too!"

Leo, who had been watching this exchange like a tennis match, his head darting back and forth, finally spoke. "We've been friends and—"

My mom cut him off. "Friends, friends. How can you be friends if I've never heard of you?"

It was time to cut off this interrogation before it led somewhere dangerous. "I didn't talk much about him. I didn't want questions."

My mother switched to speaking Polish. *"Because you knew we wouldn't want you hanging out with a Russian boy."*

I looked over at Leo. How much Polish did he understand?

"My mother was born in Warsaw," he said, a tentative smile on his face.

His Polish was a bit clunky, and it certainly didn't have the effect he hoped for.

My mom looked at me, eyes narrowed. She opened her mouth to speak, but my dad cut her off.

"So Leo, you helped Anna with the money to bail out Frankie?"

Oh. I should've told him that they knew about that.

I turned to Leo, eyes wide.

He didn't miss a beat. "That's right."

My mom scoffed. "How did you get the money? Did you use your crayons to draw a picture?"

"Is this some kind of a..." My dad paused. *"Pretty Woman* situation?"

My jaw dropped. "*Tata!*"

"What?" He grinned, hiding his face behind his champagne flute. "Because that CEO guy liked you, too, and if I'm going to sell a daughter into marriage, I want to get the best price."

Lisa, mid-sip, snorted and sputtered on her champagne. She waved off any offers of help and asked, "Tata, are you going to sell me into marriage, too?"

My dad paused, pretending to think on this, then shook his head. "No one would take you. You talk even more than Zuzia."

"Rude." She turned to me. "Who is the CEO guy?"

I waved a hand. "Nobody."

"He's a billionaire!" my mom said, arms crossed. "Zuzia met him when she was on the news with Dolly."

"Oh! Sorry, I didn't have a chance to watch that yet," Lisa said. "I will, though."

I put up a hand. "Please don't."

"I didn't get a chance to watch it either," Leo said, bumping me with his shoulder. "It seems like sparks flew."

"Yeah, maybe you should watch out, buddy." My mom took a swig of champagne. "He's taking her to *Switzerland*."

I shut my eyes. This was all just going swimmingly. "Mama, Leo is going to Switzerland with me."

She let out a harumph and turned her back to us, funneling her fury into scrubbing a dirty pan.

My dad started asking questions about Switzerland, but I kept my eyes on my mom.

I knew her silence only meant she was gathering her strength. After nearly ten minutes, she finished the dishes and spoke again.

"I wonder if I will be invited to the wedding." She mused. "*If* I even survive until then."

Ah, there it was. She'd gone from threatening Leo to threatening her own demise.

I sighed. "Mama, it's—"

She didn't even look at me, instead turning and walking out of the room.

"Excuse me," I said, following her out of the kitchen and down the hallway. She didn't stop until she got to the bathroom. I had to stick my hand in the door to get her to stop. "Mama, come on. Don't run and hide."

"Why? My heart is broken," she said, peering through the gap in the open door. "I am having a heart attack. At my funeral, do not let your *husband* put carnations on my grave."

I pried the door open. "Would you please talk to me?"

"Talk to you? The way you talked to me?"

I should have planned this better. At the same time, what could I possibly have said that would've made it okay? "He's a nice guy, and he's helping me with Frankie. I can pay for a good lawyer now."

"Is this about money, Zuzia? Is this how we taught you?"

"No, of course not."

"I thought the worst thing that could happen was one of my children going to prison, but now..." She stood, staring at me. "You lie to me, you hide what you are doing, and now you are running off with a Russian criminal."

I had to force myself to stare straight ahead so I wouldn't roll my eyes. "He's not a criminal."

She dropped her voice to a whisper. "How do you think he has money for lawyers? *Think!* Do you really believe he has money from drawing pictures?"

"He's very successful, Mama."

Her hand dropped to her side and she took a deep breath. There was a dash of flour on her cheek, ghostly white on her skin. The bags under her eyes looked especially purple and wrinkled.

When had my mother gotten so wrinkled?

I opened my mouth and she held up a hand. "Don't start." Tears filled her eyes and she turned away, resting her hands on the bathroom sink.

I stared at her, trying to come up with the right words to say, some way to fix what I'd done, undo the damage and rewind. My chest felt like it was trapped in a vice, with pressure from all sides – Frankie, and work, and Leo with those stupid flowers.

"I am scared for you, Zuzia. Ever since you told me about this, I was thinking *what can I do so my daughter doesn't have to sell herself? What can we do?* How we have failed."

Just like that, the pressure reached a crescendo, and something inside of me broke with a clear *snap.*

"It's not a real engagement, Mama."

"I know. He didn't even give you a ring."

I looked down at my hand. A detail I'd forgotten. "No, I mean...." I sighed. "I'll tell you the truth, but you can't tell anyone, Mama. I mean it. No one can know."

She looked at me, her eyes wild, the tears nearly gone. "You think I would tell anyone what you're doing?"

I stepped closer and lowered my voice. "We're not actually engaged. He's a new professor at work. He offered me a hundred thousand dollars to pretend to be his fiancé for a few months."

Her eyes softened, widening. After a moment, she asked, "Why?"

"I don't know."

"So he *is* a criminal!" she whispered. "What kind of a deal is that?"

"I don't know, but are we really going to let Frankie use the cheap lawyer his friends found? So he can sit in prison with them until he's eighty years old?"

The front door opened, the sound carrying down the hall, and within seconds, Frankie's voice called out a hello.

She looked back at me. "Do you swear you are not lying to me?"

"Yes, Mama. I swear."

She pressed her hands together, wringing them like a cartoon character. "What if he hurts you?"

I'd seriously considered this possibility, and like the women who had trusted Ted Bundy, I decided it was an impossibility.

"He's not going to hurt me. Don't worry. I threatened him." I lowered my voice. "But I'm serious. You can't tell *anyone.* Not your sisters, no family in Massachusetts, absolutely no one in Poland."

"Not even your father?"

I frowned. That was asking the impossible. "Fine. You can tell him, but *no one* else, or we will lose the money."

Her hand flew to her mouth and she bit at a fingernail.

"It's for Frankie," I said.

"For Frankie," she said, nodding. She looked over my shoulder, then back at me. "Okay. I can do it. I can keep a secret. I will not spill the balls."

I smiled, the tension dissipating from my chest. "The beans."

She cocked her head to the side. "What beans?"

"You won't spill the *beans*."

"I won't spill the beans either."

I laughed and, finally, she smiled, too.

"Don't look too happy," I said. "Everyone still has to think it's real."

"Yes, it *is* real," she said, stiffening her shoulders. "It's very bad. I'll tell your father to scare Leo more."

"He's scared," I said. "Don't worry."

She nodded at me once, then called out. "Welcome home, Frankush!" before walking down the hallway.

I took a step into the bathroom and looked in the mirror. If there was anyone who knew how important this was, it was my mom. She hadn't slept since Frankie got arrested. I could trust her. I had to trust her.

I'd told one person. That wasn't so bad.

Well, two if you counted my dad, but no one ever did. They were essentially one person, with a grumpy half and a goofy half, like all good buddy duos.

It was going to be fine. Leo wasn't going to find out I had blabbed. The lawyer would save Frankie. Everything would work out.

I took a deep breath and turned to rejoin the party.

CHAPTER TEN

Leo

F rankie's arrival shifted the focus away from me and Anna and improved the mood considerably. Anna's mom still wouldn't look at me, but after two more glasses of champagne, she managed a few smiles, mostly at Frankie's stories from jail. He had his dad's sense of humor.

"My cellmate was arrested for public indecency," he told us. "Police caught him standing outside naked."

"Just standing there?" Lisa asked. "Why?"

Frankie cracked a smile. "He was in the shower when he smelled smoke and thought his house was on fire. Ran outside, got locked out."

"Why did he run?" Stanley asked. "He was safer in the shower. He could have sprayed the fire."

"Yes," Lisa said, "because that's how fires work."

I laughed, but held back comment. I had no interest in attracting any more attention from Anna's mom. She was now entirely engrossed in Frankie's stories, though she did occasionally take an opportunity to shoot me a dirty look.

The rest of the family was curious, even welcoming, to the strange man the inscrutable Anna had brought home. Lisa kept trying to include me, and after the four-course dinner Anna's mom had served – homemade chicken soup, fried pork cutlets, mashed potatoes, mizeria, Cesar salad, and little Polish apple pies for dessert – Lisa pulled out the family photo albums.

"There is your future bride." She pointed to a brown-haired Anna, perhaps ten years old, her round face framed by straight bangs and her eyes almost disappearing as she smiled intensely. "Isn't she beautiful?"

"Adorable," I said.

"Look at that sweaty face," Anna said, shaking her head. "No wonder my parents pushed me so hard in school. They knew I wouldn't get anywhere on my looks."

Her mom gasped. "Anna! That is not true."

"We pushed you so you'd have money to take care of us when we're old," Stanley said matter-of-factly.

"I thought I was the one taking care of you," Lisa protested. "Anna doesn't make any money. She's poor."

He nodded and took a sip of his beer. "You're the backup."

"I make slightly more than the average salary for the city, thank you," Anna said, straightening in her seat.

"With only *slightly* more education," Frankie added. "And still. You're poor."

She stuck her tongue out at him.

"It's not about that, Anna" Lisa said. "It's the fact that you're happy not making any money because you're a nerd."

"I am *not* a nerd!" Anna said with a huff.

"Really? Then why do you love school like a nerd?"

Anna crossed her arms. "You're just jealous because you went into contract law and bored yourself to death."

The bickering detoured into whose schooling was more tedious, and I excused myself to go refill my water.

I didn't realize Frankie had followed me until I heard his voice.

"Hey."

I jumped, then turned to face him. "Oh, hey."

He smiled for a second, hesitating before saying, "I wanted to thank you for helping Anna. And me."

I set my water glass down. "No problem."

"Are you really an artist?"

I felt like a fraud, telling anyone I was some sort of authority, but by becoming a professor, I could talk theory and shadow into the wee hours of the morning and never have to pick up a brush again. "It seems that way."

"I like to do a little graphic design and a little drawing." He shook his head. "But I'm not good."

I smiled. He seemed like a nice kid. Too nice to have kidnapped an old couple sleeping in the back of an RV. "Humility is the first step to greatness."

"Ha, yeah." He cleared his throat. "I didn't do it, you know."

Was he reading my eyes? Maybe it had been written on my face. "You mean the RV?"

"Yeah. My friends Jamie and Brandon called me that night and said, 'Go stand outside your apartment, we've got something to show you.' I was already out there waiting for my pizza to be delivered, and they pulled up in an RV."

"Were the people in the back screaming or anything?"

"No! They didn't make a sound. I thought Jamie's parents bought the RV. They're always buying stuff. Like, they have a boat and jet skis."

"Ah. He's the jet ski friend. Is that why you kept him around? I bet he has a pool too."

A smile broke across Frankie's face. "Yeah, he does. How'd you know?"

I shrugged. "Just a feeling. Did your friends tell the cops you had nothing to do with it?"

"I don't know. I think so, but I guess the cops didn't believe them."

I could see why Anna felt the need to rescue him. She was ten years older, the same as my brother had been to me. Was that how my brother had seen me? A kid to be rescued? "Don't sweat it. I'm sure it'll work out."

"Yeah. Maybe I can take a class with you."

"You're at Madison?"

He nodded. "I missed a few weeks being in jail, though, so I might not be allowed back this semester. But maybe next semester, if I'm not..."

His voice trailed off, and before he could finish the thought, Anna rushed in. "We've gotta go. Lisa pulled out the karaoke machine and I am *not* here for it."

As if on cue, Lisa's voice cried out from the other room. "I'll let you sing the main part in *Total Eclipse of the Heart!* I'll do all the 'turn arounds!'"

She grabbed me by the hand and started pulling me back into the living room. At first, I was surprised she was touching me, then I was surprised by how strong she was, able to drag me through the house like it was nothing.

"It was a lovely party, but we have to go," she yelled. "We're leaving for Switzerland in the morning."

I nodded along, smiling, trying to not look down at her hand wrapped around mine. How could her hand be so small and full of so much fury?

"Well." Her mother stood from the couch, hands on her hips. "I hope you have a nice time, Anna."

"Thanks, Mama."

Her head snapped toward me, like a bird zeroing in on an insect. "And you."

I smiled, trying to think of something to say, but she beat me to it. "Don't do anything stupid."

I nodded. "I'll try my best."

She gave Anna a kiss on the cheek and we were off, back down the hallway with pictures of hanging shrines to each child, through the door, past the flower baskets on the porch, and into a downpour.

We ran to the minivan and shut ourselves inside, only the sound of the raindrops between us.

Anna spoke first. "I'm sorry I told them about the money for Frankie. It's just—"

I put up a hand. "No, it's fine. The best lies need to have truth to them."

"Right. Yeah." A water droplet rolled from her forehead, skipped over her eye, and splashed onto her cheek.

It almost looked like a tear, but I suspected Anna didn't cry, not even as a baby.

"Was it everything you hoped it would be?" she asked.

I turned to face straight ahead, watching as a droplet hit the windshield. For a moment it was perfect, round, unmoving, then another droplet slid into it, capturing it and taking it away. "It was better, actually."

She laughed and started the car. "I tried to warn you."

"You did."

The rain smeared makeup under her eye. Without thinking, I leaned forward to wipe it away, but stopped myself, instead diverting my hand to turn on the radio.

As intimate as meeting her family was, her mom had a point. We were still essentially strangers.

She turned to back out of the driveway. "One of Ken's many assistants sent me an email. I can forward it to you. It has our itinerary."

"Does it start with me being pushed off a mountain?"

She nodded. "How'd you know? He must be working with my mom."

I cracked a smile. "Does she ever hold back? Your mom?"

Anna paused for a moment before replying. "No. You should see when someone cuts her in line." She laughed, resulting in a little snort. "My parents can't do lines. They start to panic, like they've been transported back to communist Poland, forced to wait behind a hundred other people for a bag of random vegetables."

Sounded familiar to me. "That's understandable."

"One of these days she's going to end up on the news for throwing a fit at a line jumper."

I shifted to face her. "That reminds me, I need to watch your news segment."

"Do me a favor and don't." She tossed her phone into my hands. "Forward that email to yourself. We have to be ready tomorrow at six."

That was early. This dude really wanted to see Anna. "Quite trusting, handing me your phone like this."

She shot me a side glance. "All part of being your fiancée, dear."

I sent the email to myself and returned her phone, skimming the long message from Ken's assistant.

There were more than a few interesting bits of information. First, Ken was flying us out in one of his private planes. Not just any plane – one of his company's prototype hydrogen-hybrid planes. There was an excited paragraph about the technology involved – surely for Anna's benefit – detailing the hydrogen combustion turbines and hydrogen fuel cells.

It meant nothing to me, except the last line. "Mr. Fielding would like to extend your exclusive use of the plane for the duration of the conference."

My heart skipped a beat. A direct flight to Kraków couldn't take more than two hours on a private plane. It wasn't too late to plan a trip. I just needed to call and see if she was busy...

"Did you see there's a black-tie event at the end of the week?" Anna made a face. "A rich people ball. Maybe we can skip it."

I looked up from my phone and cleared my throat. "I don't think so, Cinderella. Not if you're supposed to schmooze for the university."

She let out a groan. "I'm no good at schmoozing."

I looked back at my phone. Anna wouldn't mind if I left for a few days. She'd have her hands full trying to escape Ken's wooing.

Or maybe she'd embrace it. Money was seductive, even if he was completely wrong for her. Once our business was done, she was free to fall into his billion-dollar-embrace.

But not before then. "I can give you some advice."

"Oh yeah? Are you good at schmoozing?"

"Unfortunately, I am."

She looked over at me. "What's the trick, then?"

"You just have to pretend like you don't hate the people you're talking to."

She laughed. "I don't hate them."

"Except you do."

"I hate having to be *fake* with them."

"You don't have to be fake."

Anna shook her head. "Only a hotshot artist who doesn't have to take crap from anyone would say something like that."

"I spent *years* listening to rich people tell me what my work was about, just so they would consider buying something." I paused. "Maybe that's my advice, then. Just listen. Don't make smart comments."

She groaned. "I don't think you understand. I can't do that."

"You can. Of course you can."

"Carl is acting like this is a great opportunity, not just for me, but for the university. I guess he thinks we could find research partners and investors?" She let out a heavy sigh. "I'm sure I will ruin it all."

"You won't ruin it. Just smile, and nod, and laugh at people's bad jokes."

"I need a coach." She turned to me. "Leo, you're the only one with experience with these kinds of people. You have to teach me."

In that moment, I saw her as she'd been in that photo album, ten years old, round-faced and full of hope. Even Anna had been a child once, and I'd meant what I'd told Lisa. She was adorable then and she is now.

"Sure."

"Awesome!" Anna turned back to the road, grinning ear to ear. "I knew you couldn't be all bad."

"Oh yeah?"

She nodded. "I told my mom I liked you, and you know what? I kind of meant it."

"Wow, you're already practicing your flattery. That was a decent start. I give it a C-minus."

"A C-minus!" she yelled. "That was at least a B."

"We'll work on it." I smiled to myself and turned to look out the window. I'd wait to tell her about my trip. No need to ruin what little goodwill I'd earned.

CHAPTER ELEVEN

Anna

The next morning, an SUV with blacked out windows pulled up outside of my apartment. I stood by my door and squinted, unsure if this was my ride or if I was about to get kidnapped.

The back window rolled down and Leo stared at me, his expression flat. "I heard a rumor."

My heart dropped into my stomach. I'd rather face a kidnapping than admit I had told my mom about our scheme.

I was barely able to croak out an, "Oh?"

His blue eyes shined even under the streetlights. "There aren't any tux rental places in Zermatt."

Coolness flushed through my chest and limbs, pulling my heart back into place. "I wouldn't have assumed there was one."

He got out of the car and held the door open. "It puts me in an awkward position. I don't own a tuxedo."

The driver got out of his seat and I said hello. He nodded, taking my bag and stowing it in the back.

How odd this all was. If anyone from my family were here to witness this spectacle, they would not be able to resist the urge to yell out, "Don't let her in the car! She's poor!"

I smiled at the thought. The *poor* name calling had escalated over the years. It started when my mom saw a movie where one character called another character poor, and whether or not it was intended to be funny, she thought it was the height of comedy, right up there with people falling down or cartoonishly stepping on rakes.

There was no one around to call me poor now except me, and I wasn't going to out myself. I slipped into the backseat of the SUV and ran my hand over the soft leather, sucking in the heavenly smell.

Did Ken just throw away cars once the new car smell wore off?

Probably. Meanwhile, my minivan smelled like someone had spilled milk into the back seat and let it rot in the sun, because they had. (My cousin Katherine, ten years ago, when she was eight).

I watched the driver shut the back door, walk around the front, and take his seat. He didn't look back at us or say anything. He must have known we didn't belong here.

Scratch that. Leo belonged. He seemed at home wherever he went, cool and unaffected, not a care in the world.

"Do you really think they meant it when they said black tie?" Leo asked, sliding into his seat.

"I do." Or at least I hoped, because I'd carefully packed a gown into a garment bag and lugged it all the way here. If it was all for nothing, I was going to scream.

The driver started the car without a word, and it dawned on me that he could be reporting everything we did back to Ken.

Was that a problem? Or did it not matter? I had no idea whom we were trying to fool, just that my mom was at home right now, wide awake, resisting (or let's be honest, not resisting) the urge to pick up the phone and tell the truth about the engagement to anyone who would listen.

The thought made me dizzy. I put a hand out to steady myself, then decided to focus on the things I could control.

I pulled out my phone and typed a text to Leo, leaning to show it to him. "I didn't think of this until now, but I guess anyone could be watching us? Even the driver?"

He leaned over, read the message, and shrugged.

I deleted the text and wrote again. "If you would tell me WHO we're pretending for, I could be less on edge."

Leo reached out, gently brushing my hand as he took the phone from me. A flutter ran down my wrist, my hand tingling where he'd made contact.

How odd. I couldn't remember the last time a guy had touched me. In a purely academic sense, I knew people weren't supposed to live without human contact. Yet, until that moment, I didn't understand why.

I crossed my arms over my chest.

"I'll tell you soon," he wrote back. "Not yet. But you're right, we need to keep up appearances."

He handed the phone back to me just as a weight pressed into my back. At first I thought something was falling onto me, but quickly realized Leo had put an arm around my shoulders.

I looked up at him. He kept his eyes straight ahead, his expression blank.

"Shouldn't you buckle your seatbelt?" I said under my breath.

He glanced down and smiled. "Nah. I trust Steve."

The driver looked at us in the rearview mirror. "Thanks, Leo. You're a doll."

They both laughed.

"He's worked for Ken for a decade," Leo said. "Ken had him drive out from Chicago to get us."

Ah. We *were* being watched, and Leo was on it.

If he was a criminal like my mom suspected, at least he was clever. Plus, he wasn't the most unpleasant to be around. He smelled nice, and the placidity he radiated, though puzzling, could be calming.

The muscles in my back and shoulders sunk under the weight of Leo's arm, forcing whatever tension I'd been carrying to dissipate. Between the chilly morning and my nerves about the trip, I'd felt cold since I'd woken up. Leo was warm, and I no longer felt like I was about to break into a shiver.

What I'm saying is it wasn't the worst feeling in the world, and for the sake of our ruse, there was no need to break away, so I didn't. That's all. I wasn't at risk of falling in love with him, or how he'd put it, "getting emotional."

There wasn't much traffic, and we glided through street after street without hitting a red light. I stared out the window, watching the sleepy morning pass by as the sun began its rise. I could have leaned over and rested my head on his chest, but I didn't. That would've been too far, and the only time I took things too far was when I made jokes, told stories, or ended up on the local news.

It was odd being chauffeured around. Every trip I'd ever taken involved me being the circus ringleader, reminding my siblings when we had to leave, checking and double checking to make sure no one had forgotten anything important, and organizing the details down to the last sandwich.

Being the eldest of four was like being a second mother, or maybe an aunt – not the fun, drunk aunt, but the stern one, the one who had to enforce bedtime and make healthy dinners and while she was too young to go as the parent to parent-teacher conferences, she was too old to slap the spitting-gum-in-the-hair bully on Lisa's bus, even though she *really* wanted to.

There was no one to chase around today. The plan today was to fly out of some little municipal airport, which I suspected was another rich person thing that would make me uncomfortable.

We got there quickly, and I wasn't entirely wrong in my prediction. The building didn't look like much – it could've passed for a library if not for the small sign with a plane on it – but just beyond the parking lot stood a sleek private jet shining in the morning sun. It was entirely white, save for the tips of the wings, which were blue and bent vertically, pointing to the sky.

I was gawking when Steve opened the door and a man in an all-white suit rushed to meet us.

"Dr. Makowski," he said, taking off his white hat, "I'll be your pilot today. It's a pleasure to have you flying with us."

Why did he match the plane!

I extended a handshake, trying not to stare at the little blue flourishes on his shoulders or on his patent leather white shoes.

"Nice looking airplane," Leo said, shaking his hand.

"Thank you, sir." He turned and began walking along a path to the runway. "We can take off as soon as you're ready."

Leo looked over his shoulder and mouthed, "*Sir*."

To my bewilderment, Steve got my bags out of the car and started rolling them toward the plane.

"I can take that," I called out, trying to pry the rolling suitcase from his very large hand.

"Please, allow me," he said, tightening his grip. "I have instructions to make sure your every need is met."

"That's horrifying," I blurted out, tugging at the handle. The suitcase didn't budge. "It's really okay. I can carry my bag."

He was a brick wall, staring at me, and Leo interrupted. "Come on, honey. Let the man do his job."

Now *that* I didn't like. I stopped to glare at him, but he was already moving, his bag slung over his shoulder, his eyes surely laughing at me.

I was being moved around like Travel Barbie, from a car to a plane and then who knows where, except my hair didn't look as perfect and my luggage wasn't pink. It was black, like the pit in my stomach where I kept all my lies.

What was I supposed to do? Turn around and go home?

That was an extremely appealing option, but with my career hanging in the balance, I instead gritted my teeth and followed them onto the runway. The plane was waiting, its door open, white stairs ready to whisk us to luxury.

It was such bourgeois flying. No security, no shoe removal dance. My every need being met.

Shudder.

Leo reached the plane first and turned to wait for me.

"After you," he said with a smile.

I gave him a nod and walked up the stairs, two flight attendants greeting me as I entered the cabin. It was a bit nicer than your average flight, with white leather couches lining the left side and a polished wooden bar on the right. There was a TV above the bar stocked with intricate bottles, and toward the back there were more plush leather seats and tables.

I scooted to the back, dragging my enormous purse along with me. The paper Carl and I had submitted finally came back with comments, and the sooner I could get through them, the better.

I sat down and set up a workstation with my laptop and coffee mug. Leo took the seat next to me as one of the flight attendants appeared, a perky blue hat perched atop her head.

"Welcome to the Fielding-in-flight prototype. We'll start the in-air service with a glass of Krug Grande Cuvée." She held out a tray with two bubbling champagne glasses.

How much champagne was I going to have to drink this week? I didn't even like the stuff, but I couldn't refuse it now and look uncouth.

I accepted a glass. "Thank you."

"Do you have any vintage Dom Perignon?" Leo asked.

"Of course, sir. We have a 1959 vintage, will that do?"

He nodded. "I'll try a glass."

When she disappeared through a door in the back, I turned to him. "What was that about?"

He leaned his head in and dropped his voice. "I didn't want Ken thinking he can serve us the cheap stuff."

I took a sip. It didn't taste cheap. It tasted like it cost more than my rent.

The flight attendant returned, leaving a glass and a large bottle for Leo and alerting us to the menus on the table.

Once she disappeared, I nodded toward the bottle. "How much do you think that costs?"

"Bit over two grand." He took a sip. "Yeah, still don't like champagne."

I suppressed a laugh. "Why'd you ask for it then?"

"If Ken is going to so flagrantly try to steal you away from me, I have to get my revenge somehow."

Interesting. "I thought you weren't the jealous type, Leo."

"I'm not. Usually I'm relieved when a girlfriend loses interest in me. It lets me off the hook before things get messy." He pushed the menu out of the way and set his glass down.

"Well." I sat back. "No wonder you had to pay for a girlfriend."

"You're not my girlfriend, Dr. Makowski. You're my doting fiancée."

"Don't push it." I set my nearly empty champagne glass down. Why was I drinking this early in the morning? Shouldn't there be a splash of orange juice in there to make it acceptable? What were these rich people doing to me?

"What do you mean 'before things get messy?'" I asked. "Have you been killing these women?"

He laughed. "No. I mean, you know. Messy with feelings."

"Their feelings? Or yours."

"Theirs, of course. I'm Russian, I don't have feelings, didn't you know?" He downed the rest of his glass. "Speaking of feelings, we need to talk about your mom."

His words hit me in the chest and pushed all the air out of my lungs. He knew! He knew I'd told her and he'd been waiting until I was trapped to confront me!

How could it have gotten back to him so quickly? My mother's gossip should only be crossing the Atlantic right now, and with the time change, it wouldn't have had time to get back to US soil.

I tried acting cool, opening my email and staring at the computer screen, but ended up coughing on a bit of spit I'd sucked into my throat in terror.

"Easy there," he said, patting me on the back.

There was that touch again. Did he realize he was doing it? Or was he just a flirt?

"Sorry," I said, patting my chest.

"Didn't mean to scare you."

I shook my head. Now that I'd started the lie, I had to keep it going. I had a lie going with my mom, and a lie with him, and was I lying to Ken and Carl, too, and what was this even about? I'd woven a web of lies, and now I was stuck in the middle, waiting to be crushed.

I swallowed, clearing my throat. "What do you want to know?"

"I don't know. Just – what's her story?"

Oh.

My lies were safe for now. I crawled down from my web, relief washing over me in waves.

I really needed to stop telling people about the engagement being fake, and I had to stop talking so much in general. I knew this. I accepted it.

Being aware of my flaws didn't stop me from also being woefully unable to control them, though, and I talked for the entirety of takeoff and the first hour of the flight.

I blathered on and on, telling Leo how my mom had been in her last year of medical school when she and my dad won lottery visas to the US, how they'd decided to run off together and get married. How she'd planned to finish school here but got pregnant with me, and when they had no money, her temporary job as a maid became permanent, and she eventually started a cleaning company of her own.

On and on I went, all the way to my teenager-hood, telling him how I'd spent my free time helping with my mom's fledgling business.

"You must've hated it," Leo said. "Cleaning toilets while your friends went to the mall."

"My mom doesn't believe in friends." I smiled, preparing my best impression of her. "'Less friends, more studying.'"

"Is this your way of telling me you had no friends?"

I narrowed my eyes. "I *had* friends. I just happened to also be really good at cleaning bathrooms."

"I'm sure the other kids didn't let you forget it."

Hm. He seemed to be listening, and despite his claims, he did understand feelings. Perhaps he preferred to put all his feelings into his art, locking them in oil, pretending they didn't exist. "The other kids didn't know until the time my mom brought me to clean my nemesis Nikki's house."

"You had no friends *and* a nemesis?" He sat back and shook his head. "This sounds like the making of a villain."

"Again, I had friends, and they hated Nikki, too. Her parents had this huge house – eight bedrooms, even though it was just the three of them – and right when my mom and I pulled up, I told her I couldn't go in."

"Which she respected, I'm sure."

I smiled. "She told me she couldn't clean it herself, no one would see me, and to stop being dramatic."

"I've heard about you being dramatic before."

Ah. Right. I never should've let him meet my family. I should have hired actors. Why hadn't I thought of it until now?

I went on. "Nikki was home, of course, and followed me around the entire time, making messes, because she's a terrible person. She opened a can of glitter and dumped it on a tile floor. Where do you even get a *can* of glitter?"

"At the terrible person store."

"Oh, your favorite store?"

He nodded. "Correct."

"The next day at school, she told everyone my family was living out of a van, and that her parents had hired me to be a servant."

He made a face. "Dang. She really was a terrible person."

This is where I should've stopped talking. Actually, I should've stopped an hour ago, but this also would have been a good time.

Yet I went on.

"That's not the point of this, though. You asked about my mom. She doesn't take things lying down."

"I can see that."

"When I got picked on as a kid..." I paused. Did I need to tell him how they called me weenie face? Did he need to know about that?

No, I could keep that to myself.

I cleared my throat. "I told my parents about being bullied, and my dad told me to ignore the other kids, but my mom proposed rules for a first-grader fight club. She told me I wasn't allowed to hit anyone first, but if they started it, I wouldn't get in trouble for defending myself."

He raised an eyebrow. "Is this your way of telling me you killed your nemesis?"

"No, I'm not you." He chuckled and I went on. "I told everyone about the locked room in her house filled with doll replicas of her friends and all the popular guys at school."

Leo stared at me. "What? Was that real? Or did you make it up?"

"Of course I made it up. Everyone believed it. Nikki then tried to get me banned from the eighth-grade formal, but instead got iced out of the committee." I sat back. "Some of my best work, really."

Leo stared, speechless, and the uncomfortable silence between us was broken only when a flight attendant stopped by to ask if we were ready to eat.

"I'd love to," he said, then turned to me. "Anna Doll?"

The overshare was complete. Embarrassment, my oldest friend, settled in, and I sunk into the luxurious chair.

Maybe this was how we fixed our flaws? By repeatedly cutting ourselves on them, over and over, until we finally got the message?

I made up my mind to not tell him another long, boring story for the remainder of the trip and forced a smile. "I should get back to work."

CHAPTER TWELVE

Leo

The plane descended into the mountains, slipping beneath the clouds as effortlessly as a dolphin in the waves.

Anna was busy with her work, furiously typing on her laptop and scribbling in a notebook. Despite the lavish dinner they'd served – canapés of marinated feta and poached lobster, followed by Charolais beef in a white wine and Perigueux sauce, a cheese sampling and white chocolate coffee truffles – she'd hardly eaten a thing.

"Are you feeling all right?" I'd asked after polishing off my fifth truffle.

She didn't even look up. "Yes, just busy."

I didn't want to bother her, so I turned to watch as we went deeper into the mountains, the sun disappearing behind the jagged peaks. The clouds made for a brilliant sunset, echoing the dark blue and violets with dazzling orange and gold splashes, the warm red hues bursting out before the night would envelop us in darkness.

It was the first time I'd truly noticed any beauty in the colors around me since my brother had died. The world had turned grey for so long.

Maybe it was Anna. She was different than my friends back home. In the city, everyone was an aspiring artist or aspiring model or actor, or, or, or. Everyone had a hustle, an urge to climb, and people simply did not say no to free lobster canapés.

Anna was the opposite of that. She had to be practically coerced to attend one of the most exclusive meetings in the world, and she was so thoroughly unimpressed by this private plane that I *almost* felt bad for Ken.

She was continuously surprising, but still, Ken would win in the end. I knew that. My last girlfriend had left me for an investment banker. Money talked, and Ken was made of the stuff. That and his insatiable need for *more*. He didn't even know Anna, but the fact that she was both taken and difficult to impress made her irresistible. For a man who had everything, she was a conquest. I was just a complication.

A complication with unlimited access to his plane. I had already spoken to the pilot and confirmed he was at "our" disposal for the week. If everything went well on my trip to Kraków, I decided I would tell Anna what our arrangement was all about. Maybe if she understood how important it was, she'd delay riding off into the sunset with Ken for a few weeks.

The plane dipped, preparing for landing, and Anna tucked her laptop back into her bag.

"Did you finish?" I asked.

She startled at the sound of my voice. "What?"

"Sorry. Finish with the comments on your paper."

Anna yawned, covering her mouth before answering. "Almost. I want to read it over one more time before I send it to Carl."

"Very nice."

"What have you been doing?"

I sighed and held up the book cover on my phone. "Reading *Water for Elephants* on your recommendation."

"Huh. And what do you think so far?"

"It's better than the last book I read to impress a girl." I slipped the phone back into my pocket. "*Twilight.*"

She laughed. "Team Edward?"

"Of course. How'd you know?"

She yawned again, leaning forward to stretch her arms and back. "The moody, brooding thing fits your persona."

"You don't seem the type to read teenage vampire romances."

"Wasn't my idea. It was my dad's. He insisted."

"*Your* dad?"

"He's the most well-read elevator technician in the country." She shook her head, a smile lingering on her face. "Normally he sticks to the classics, but he heard how popular *Twilight* was and had to try it. He liked it so much he made me read it too."

My father would never read *Twilight*. He never read anything for pleasure, and probably hadn't cracked a joke since before I was born. What was it like to have a father as astonishing and hilarious as hers?

Before I could ask, the pilot announced we were free to disembark and Anna stood.

"Ready for more rich people showing off?"

I nodded. "Always."

We stepped off the plane and were greeted by a navy sky. Dusk had arrived in a hurry, and a car waited for us on the runway.

"Just one more hour to Zermatt," the driver assured us. "Mr. Fielding is eagerly awaiting your arrival."

"I bet he is," I said quietly.

Anna ignored me.

This driver was far chattier than Steve, asking where we were from, if we liked to travel, and where we liked to ski.

Anna did most of the talking. "I've never skied before."

"No!" The driver gasped. "How can it be?"

"My mother always said it was dangerous." She dropped her voice. "And expensive."

I was going to respond, but the driver took over the conversation, telling us how Switzerland had the finest skiing in the world, the most beautiful mountains, the best food and, of course, the friendliest people.

We drove into the sleepy town of Zermatt listening to tales from his school days. Quaint villas lined the streets, their roofs blanketed in snow. The entire town was tucked beneath the snowy mountains, aglow with warm, cozy lights.

Our hotel was only a few minutes away, down a quiet road at the foot of the mountain.

"Welcome to paradise," the driver declared before rushing out of his seat to open the door.

Anna stepped out first. "It's stunning."

I followed her and looked up at the grand building. It looked a bit like a castle, with pointed peaks and tall windows, luminescent in the night. Surrounding the building were smaller, three-story chalets with balconies covered in twinkling lights.

"I suppose it'll do," I said, soliciting no reaction from my travel partner.

A team of four bellhops loaded our bags onto a cart as a sharply dressed woman in a cream suit strode toward us.

"Welcome to Helvetii Palace!" She extended a hand. "I'm the manager and will serve as your personal liaison."

Anna accepted her hand with a smile. "Grüezi!"

"Oh my goodness. Ken warned me you were charming." She wagged a finger. "Come, follow me."

She had the air of a cheerful schoolteacher, and intent on not disappointing, we immediately walked after her.

"And you said you don't know how to schmooze," I said as we walked into the lobby.

The floor was marble, with white columns reaching to the twenty-foot vaulted white ceilings. Above us hung a sparkling crystal chandelier, and straight ahead was the only color in the room, a towering sculpture of a tree. The bark was blown red glass, and every leaf hanging from the branches was a different color of stained glass.

"It's not schmoozing, it's being polite," she said quietly.

"Baby steps."

The manager led us to an elevator with cast iron doors, the gold, black, and rose woven into intricate patterns. "Ken sends his apologies; he is stuck with last-minute planning for the conference."

"It's no problem," Anna said.

The elevator doors opened and she waved us inside. "Dinner has already been served for the evening, but I am happy to send whatever you desire to your room."

"Thank you." Anna stepped in. "We're fine."

I cleared my throat. "Anna's very hungry."

She rushed to correct me. "I'm not."

The woman smiled and hit the button for floor five. "You have full access to the spa and the indoor pools. Please do not hesitate to contact me—I've provided my personal number here."

She handed us each a business card. I was eyeing it when I looked up and noticed Anna giving me a dirty look. I tucked it into my pocket as we stepped out of the elevator and into a short hallway.

"We have you in our best suite. In the morning, you'll find you have a stunning view of the Matterhorn, which you can enjoy from one of the three balconies. The balcony off the second bedroom has an infinity hot tub that is comfortable even on the coolest nights."

She unlocked the room and pushed the door open, revealing a central room with towering windows, plush cream furniture, and muted walls. In the center of the room was an enormous bouquet of flowers in a tall red vase.

Our bags had somehow already made it to the room. The bellboys must've thrown them through the windows.

"I will allow you to get settled, but before I go, is there *anything* I can do? Anything at all?"

I opened my mouth to speak, but Anna cut me off. "No. You've been so helpful, thank you. This is beyond anything I could have imagined."

She smiled, nodded once, and left, the door shutting behind her.

"Not the nicest room, but I'll try to make the best of it," I said, turning to see Anna's reaction.

She either didn't hear or chose to ignore me. She was studying the flowers, reading a card left at the base. After a moment, she let out a little laugh and set it down.

"Are these the sort of flowers your mom expected?" I reached out, touching one of the many roses. It was a monster, half the size of my hand.

"It would've been a better start," she said, leaning in and taking a sniff.

She wandered off into one of the bedrooms, and I grabbed the card.

Dear Anna,

Welcome to Zermatt! The conference is lucky to have you, and I am delighted you are here. I am a quarter Polish on my father's side, and like you, Catholic, so I

took the liberty of assuming you would prefer separate bedrooms until your nuptials with Leo are finalized.
I'll be in touch soon, but please enjoy everything Zermatt has to offer!

Yours,
Ken

"Hey Anna," I called out. "I have this funny feeling Kenny is trying to separate us."

She popped her head out from behind a door. "You think?"

Finally, a smile. "He's not the most subtle man."

"I'm not the most subtle woman." She tapped her chin as though lost in thought. "On the other hand, isn't it fun to watch how someone reacts to not getting what they want?"

"It is."

She smiled, tossing a booklet into my hands. "Look at the lectures for this conference. *Opportunities in Recession. Wars of the Future. Securing Water Futures.*"

I flipped through the pages, skimming over pictures of mountains and laughing models. "The water one is for you."

"Sounds gross."

I cleared my throat. Now seemed as good a time as any. I handed the booklet back to her. "Sadly, I'm going to miss all of the talks."

"What?" Anna peered up at me. "You are not making me go through this alone."

"You're not alone. You have Ken."

She narrowed her eyes.

"I really am sorry," I said, "but I have to go to Kraków."

"Right now?"

I nodded. "Can't let Ken's plane sit and rot."

Anna crossed the room, taking a seat on the white chaise lounge and drawing her knees up to her chest.

She looked tiny on that enormous thing. I felt a flash of guilt. "I thought you'd be happy to have me out of your hair."

She shrugged.

"Are you angry with me?"

"No, it's just..." She sighed. "Now I have to try to make a conference friend. There's nothing worse than wandering around a conference by yourself."

Oh.

I took a seat across from her. "You'll be fine. You're charming, remember?"

"That was the only Swiss-German word I know. My charm ran out the moment we walked into this place."

"I've got it." I clapped my hands together. "Learn some more words."

She rocked her head from side to side, considering this. Finally, she pointed a finger at me. "Fine, but you'd better be here to help me schmooze on Friday. You promised."

I suppressed a smile. She was right — it was interesting watching someone react to not getting what they wanted.

Always surprising, that Anna.

"I wouldn't miss it for the world."

CHAPTER THIRTEEN

Anna

My morning started off sluggish, and it took me a minute to realize Leo had snuck out while I was sleeping.

Rude.

It was fine for him to fly off to Poland. Really, I didn't need him, and he didn't owe me anything except a payment once this fiancée farce was through.

However, he was not fulfilling his half of the deal in coming here. He was supposed to be my Ken repellant, and his absence made me more of a target for my admirer. Or stalker. Stalking admirer.

Was that what Ken was, an admirer? At the risk of flattering myself, it seemed possible. If not, what exactly did he want from me? Was he hoping I'd insult him again?

After the luxury flight, the indulgent room, and the ridiculous flowers, I was less inclined to be reflexively rude, but I could work something out if he was so inclined.

Was he hoping I'd change my mind and decide he was a swell guy?

That wasn't going to happen. I meant what I'd said about him and his buddies sucking the lifeblood out of every societal institution they could get their hands on. I'd bet he'd drain Lake Michigan if he thought it might make him a billion more dollars.

Because that was *just* what he needed! A billion more dollars! The billions he already had weren't enough.

Doesn't money start to lose its meaning at some point, like when you say a word too many times and it stops making sense? Did any part of Ken's life make sense?

Certainly not the part where he had brought me here. If he had a crush on me, he would be sorely disappointed. I had even less interest in dating him than I did a man with a normal level of greed.

And if he'd brought me here to get me to do a take-backsies on what I'd said?

Ha!

There was no way. Take-backsies were for something you didn't mean, like when Lisa told me I'd look like a pug if I got bangs. (She clarified I'd be a cute pug, but a pug nevertheless.)

Take-backsies were not for CEOs of hedge funds and private equity firms who could not be satisfied with having most of the money, instead making it their life's work to get *all* of the money. The lack of foresight or guilt or humanity as they destroyed everything – from hospitals to emergency vets to local housing markets – that was the only impressive thing about them. The soullessness of it all. Consumption above everything.

Even if I didn't want Ken's money, the university would gladly accept it, and then probably name a building after him.

I'd just have to try to avoid him. There was no other way, and after all, this was supposed to be a work trip.

Carl had already responded to my email about the paper. He planned to send his comments by the end of the week, and offered his customary peppy advice: *If you happen to meet someone interested in our little corner of hydrology, great, but try not to worry. What an experience you're having! Make friends! Have fun!*

How could I have fun being catered to like some sort of princess? Every time someone insisted on doing something for me, I got nauseated, like my insides were so embarrassed they were trying to crawl out of my skin.

Make friends, he says. With whom? All the speakers had titles like global director, executive director, chief executive officer of this or that company, or minister of social this or foreign that.

I decided to ignore Carl's advice and hide. That first day, I attended six talks and managed to avoid speaking to anyone until dinner that evening.

I was sitting alone at an embarrassingly large table when Ken approached me.

"I'm so sorry we haven't been able to connect until now," he said.

I waved a hand. "It's no problem. You're busy."

He was wearing a tight, tailored navy-blue suit and greeted me with a disarmingly earnest smile. I told myself it was the sort of smile you'd see on the guy who'd just auctioned off your foreclosed home, but I had to admit he was sort of handsome.

He took the seat across from me. "How are you feeling?"

Like I could collapse face-first into my soup from exhaustion, but lies were more polite. "Oh, good. Very good."

"And Leo?"

I set my spoon down. "He had to attend to some business."

Ken nodded, loosening his tie and unbuttoning the top button of his shirt. "We tried to put together an impressive first day, but I'm sure the topics aren't as academic as you're used to."

He wasn't wrong. At engineering conferences, people presented data on glacier meltwater erosion or argued about remineralization techniques.

This conference had a distinct lack of data – or at least a lack of good data. Each talk was an hour-long thesis on someone's opinion, unsupported by anything. While that was fine, it was unnerving when the attendees lined up to agree without question. There was no debate, no discussion. Just compliance.

I was supposed to be polite, though. The best I could come up with was, "It's different, but interesting."

"Tomorrow there's a talk on actionable hydrology I think you might enjoy." He pulled out a program booklet, setting it on the table before pointing to a lecture. "The presenter works as an engineer at a startup. I think you two might get along."

I skimmed her biography. She worked at a company that created devices to turn wastewater into drinking water during natural disasters.

Dang, okay. That was cool.

"Actually..." He stood up and waved a hand. "That's her there. Joanna!"

She caught sight of him, a smile brightening her face before she changed course to walk toward us. Her brown hair was in a neat ponytail, and she looked cute in a blazer and bell-bottomed white pants. I immediately wanted to know where she'd gotten her outfit.

"Hello, hello!" she said, carrying a plate loaded with food. "Excuse me for being a pig, the time change has me starved."

I smiled. It seemed like she might be my kind of woman, even though travel has the opposite effect on my appetite.

I have what my dad liked to call "a nervous stomach monster." Once, when I was six, we were flying (standby, naturally), and the monster attacked just before takeoff. I tried to get out of my seat to use the lavatory, but a flight attendant pushed me back down and told me I had to wait.

It was one of the few times I've seen my dad get angry. I remember him bellowing the phrase, "Keep your hands off my daughter," and the in-flight crisis was averted when he blocked the aisle and allowed me to run off.

"Joanna, this is Dr. Anna Makowski. She's an engineer at Madison University and specializes in hydrology."

Joanna tried to balance the plate on her arm to shake my hand. "So nice to meet you."

"You too."

"Another engineer." She dropped her voice. "Finally, someone I can talk to instead of these weirdos."

I laughed, and Joanna stuck out her tongue before jabbing Ken. "Except you, of course."

He grinned. "Sure."

"You're easy to talk to." She sat down and took a bite of bread, talking with her mouth full. "I thought engineers were bad, but some of these people seem like they crawled out from under a rock and haven't spoken to another human in decades." She shook her head.

"Guilty," Ken said, holding up a hand. "I put my foot in my mouth in front of Anna and I still haven't recovered."

His dark brown eyes lingered for a moment, reminding me how badly I was doing at my mission of hiding. I looked away.

Had he really been embarrassed? Until this moment, it was easy to think of him as the caricature I'd seen on the news screen – but was he, in fact, a real person?

"Don't worry about it," I assured him. "I say dumb things all the time. It's actually a hobby of mine."

Joanna sputtered out a laugh. "A hobby. That's a good one. What dumb thing did you say, Ken?"

He scratched the back of his head, his cheeks flushed pink. "Well..."

My goodness, still embarrassed?

He took a deep breath and went on, shaking his head. "I got a bit too excited about our new project and blathered on and—" A woman approached, whispering something urgent in his ear.

His expression faded into a frown and he looked back at us. "Please excuse me. One of the guests took a trip onto the roof, and he's refusing to come down unless I come gaze at the stars with him."

I looked at Joanna, which was a mistake. Her face made me laugh, and then she burst into laughter, too.

"Not a weird thing to do at all," she said with a snort.

"What's weird about a little bit of stargazing?" Ken rolled his eyes, then, for the briefest moment, smiled at me. "Enjoy your evening."

He left, taking long strides across the dining room. He was tall enough that he didn't look like he was rushing. Or perhaps all the money gave him poise. I didn't know.

"He's a hoot." Joanna took another bite of bread. "How did you two meet?"

He was out of sight now, a team of people with clipboards running after him.

I took a sip of water. "I insulted him on TV."

Her laughter rolled out, loud and boisterous and full. "It's good he has a sense of humor."

"How do you know him?"

"He's invested millions into our company. At first, I thought he was just another guy looking for publicity, but he's actually involved. He cares. He wants us to succeed."

"I don't mean this in a rude way," I said, "but that's surprising."

"Isn't it?" She took a bite of the salmon, her mouth entirely full. "What about you? Are you teaching at Madison?"

"I'm a post doc, hoping to get a tenure position."

"Ah. I tried that back in the day." She sighed. "The only jobs were on the other side of the country, and even then there's no guarantee of getting tenure, as you know."

Oh, I knew. "Do you like the startup?"

"I love it. Without boring you, I can say it's the most fun I've had at a job, or in my life."

"That's not boring at all." I leaned in, a grin on my face. "Tell me everything."

And so began my friendship with the amazing Joanna. My exhaustion slipped away and we spent the next two hours chatting in the hot tub in my room.

The next morning, we had breakfast together before heading into the lectures.

The only talk worth its salt was hers, and she and I got into a lively debate during the Q&A. It spurred other attendees to ask questions – some quite good – and I would have stayed to listen to them if my phone wasn't blowing up with text messages.

The first was from one of my many cousins. "Congratulations! I can't believe you kept it a secret so long!"

"He's a lucky man," wrote my uncle.

From an unknown number: "Heard you got engaged. Ha, sorry I was out of touch. Lost my phone."

Most concerning, a cousin in Buffalo. "Amazing news. We will definitely see you at the party!"

Party? What party? There were fourteen messages about a party, with everyone saying they were coming.

Coming? Coming where?

I was too afraid to ask, but deep down, I knew the answer. To add insult to injury, all this time I thought I hadn't heard from Leo because my phone didn't have service, but no. It was working fine. Leo was just ignoring me. Not to be dramatic, but he was probably off committing crimes I'd have to explain to INTERPOL when I tried to leave the country.

I'd face that later. Maybe Ken would help. He seemed to like me.

I typed out a text to my mom. "Mama, what is this I'm hearing about a party? Is this a joke?"

I paced to the bathroom and back before she answered. "Just a little party to celebrate your engagement! Smart, huh?"

Without realizing it, I groaned, and Joanna appeared out of nowhere.

"Are you okay?"

I tucked my phone into my pocket. "Yeah. Just family stuff."

"I was worried I offended you during my talk."

"Not at all. I didn't want to hog all the questions."

"What?" She grabbed me by the shoulders. "If it weren't for you, I don't think anyone would have said anything, and I would've felt like I gave a total dud talk. So thank you."

"You're welcome," I said, patting her hands, "I'm glad I was able to play such an important role with so little effort. I'll take credit for everything."

She collapsed into me, laughing, and I broke down, too. I expected she was relieved to be done, and my laughter was fueled by hearing her.

That and maybe the terror of avoiding whatever my mom was planning.

We attended every lecture together for the next three days, at which point she broke the news she was leaving early.

I'll admit. I got whiny.

"You can't go!" I told her. "The stupid black-tie dinner is tomorrow, and I might not have anyone to talk to."

"That's not true," she said, shaking her head. "That defense contractor was really interested in talking to you about how to remove toxins from civilian water supplies, which was *totally* hypothetical."

"That was unnerving." I shuddered. "His breath smelled, too. Like barbeque moth balls. It was hot but weak, like an old hair dryer that sparks sometimes and singes your hair and—"

She held up a hand. "Please stop."

"Sorry."

"I'd love to stay, but I have to get home to my little monsters or my heart will fall out of my chest." She held up her phone. "Aren't they just the worst?"

It was a picture of her son and daughter, four and two years old, sitting in a Power Wheels Jeep. Both of them had on black sunglasses, and her son had his long legs sticking straight out of the car like a baby giraffe.

I snatched the phone from her. I'd seen a lot of pictures of them over the last few days, but this one took the cake. "Can I come with you?"

"Sure! They'd love you."

"Deal."

"Seriously, though. Come visit!"

"I will."

I meant it. She was incredible, and somehow the kids seemed even cooler than her.

. . .

The evening was lonely without her, and Friday was light on lectures. I still hadn't heard from Leo, and I decided to occupy my mind by spending the afternoon at the indoor pool.

When I first got there, I was informed that my room included unlimited spa services. While a massage sounded nice in theory, the idea of a stranger touching me was too much.

Instead, I spent my time swimming laps, then relaxing in the jacuzzi as two attendees discussed how they'd bring peace to the Middle East.

After half an hour, they were satisfied they'd figured it out, and I was ready to take my leave. I got out of the jacuzzi and the spa manager rushed to greet me with a towel, insisting I use at least one of the spa services, as to not make her look bad in front of Ken.

I relented and accepted a manicure before rushing out, then fled to my room. Before going inside, I stood outside the door, listening.

Nothing but silence.

My heart dropped. Leo wasn't coming back. I was a fool to think he'd uphold his end of the bargain. I unlocked the door and pushed it open.

"Long time no see."

I screamed, not even covering my mouth. "How did you sneak in?"

Leo put his hands up. "I have a key, remember?"

His hair was tamed, recently trimmed, and he was dressed in a black tuxedo and a black bow tie.

I pulled the spa robe tightly over my chest. "I thought you didn't have a tux."

"I picked one up." He looked down. "Will it do?"

He must have had the measurements of a male model, because the tuxedo was perfect, sleek and elegant, dancing along his biceps and tailored at the waist.

I gawked at him, acutely aware of my wet hair and the strong-smelling oil they'd insisted on using to massage my hands.

"It'll do." I nodded, taking a step past him.

"Good."

I paused, turning to look at him. I'd convinced myself I'd never see him again, but there he was, looking like he'd walked out of a Bond movie. Maybe this night wouldn't be so bad after all.

"You look nice," I said, turning before he could react.

CHAPTER FOURTEEN

Leo

The guy at the tuxedo shop may as well have been a butcher, stuffing me into this thing like a sausage into a casing. It was too tight, *way* too tight, but it was the only tuxedo in the little shop, and he knew I was desperate enough to buy it.

And buy it I did. I looked down, running a finger along the satin, the material barely able to lay flat against my chest.

At least Anna was happy.

I looked up, pushing my shoulders back. "Did you decide which dress you're wearing?"

She stopped in the doorway of her bedroom, calling over her shoulder, "I only brought one dress."

"Oh." I realized I was blocking her view. I stepped aside and swooped a hand behind me. "I thought you'd seen these. Ken had them delivered."

Anna stared at the array of dresses for a moment, her face stern, before breezing past me, the smell of delicate vanilla trailing behind. Even in a white robe and slippers, she managed to look elegant.

I should tell her to just wear the robe. That would go over well.

I kept quiet as she studied Ken's dresses. One was a dazzling white gown with a large cascading bow off the shoulder. Another was a deep sapphire ballgown, crowding out a third made of rosette-colored silk, with a plunging neckline and long-sleeved beaded cuffs.

She would look beautiful in any of them, and while I was no dress expert, I was certain this collection cost more than a new car.

"Ken sent these?" she asked, touching the beading on the nearest dress.

I nodded. "There was no note, but the woman delivering them wanted you to know they're yours to keep."

Anna dropped the sleeve. "He must think I don't have any dresses of my own."

I laughed. She was unbelievable. "I'm sure he doesn't think that."

Anna stared at them, her mouth a firm line across her face. "It's like he thinks I'm a doll to dress up."

That was precisely how Ken saw her. It didn't mean she couldn't enjoy something nice, though. "You don't like the dresses?"

"I didn't say that." She kicked off her slippers and started walking back to her room.

"Are you going to try them on?"

She turned to face me. "No, they're all yours. I think the pink one will complement your skin tone."

With that, she disappeared into her room and shut the door. A moment later, the shower started.

I shook my head and sat down, unbuttoning the jacket constricting my ribcage. I'd talked to her for less than five minutes and she'd already left me dumbfounded.

It was hilarious, in a way. Anna wasn't playing hard to get; she *was* hard to get. Impossible to get and entirely insusceptible to charm.

Ken dug himself deeper with every move. Where was he now? Waiting at the bottom of a staircase for his princess to appear, all bashful and blushing?

He'd chosen the wrong princess. I sat back on the couch and covered my mouth, laughing.

Something jabbed me in the back, and when I determined it wasn't the tux tearing at the seams, I reached back and retrieved the offender: my cell phone.

The morning I'd left for Kraków, I realized it was missing just as I walked out the door. I had looked for it, but I had to be quiet as to not wake Anna, and after a few minutes, I gave up. I never would've found it in the couch.

In Kraków, the pilot had arranged for a brand-new phone to be delivered to me. I almost hated to go back to my old phone.

I heard the water shut off and stood from my seat. "Hey, Anna," I yelled through the door, "Do you think Ken would track me on the phone his pilot gave me?"

There was no response, but I could hear her moving around. I was about to repeat myself when she yelled back, "Yes. Definitely."

I knew she was right. I'd even chosen to make a two-hour drive from the airport, rather than have the pilot fly closer, in order to avoid Ken's watchful gaze. The man hated me, and as much as I, like all artists, relished hate, there was no need to risk it now.

Back on the couch, I transferred the pictures from my trip, then deleted everything from the new phone. I was tempted to leave a single picture, one of me and Anna, just for Ken to find later...

I waited on the couch, excited to tell Anna my idea. After half an hour, her door opened, and I jumped up like a kid who was about to lay a whoopie cushion.

"Hey, I thought it'd be funny to—"

I caught sight of Anna and lost my train of thought. She was wearing a black gown with delicate embroidered flowers at the bust, elegant splashes of white and yellow fading into green hanging leaves at the bottom. Her hair cascaded to her shoulders in loose curls, and her eyes shined, outlined with tones of dark brown and glittering gold at the corners.

I couldn't stop myself from saying, "You look stunning."

She clasped her hands, interlocking her fingers for a moment. "Thank you. Borrowed the makeup from my sister." She glanced at Ken's gowns, then looked back at me. "What were you saying?"

"Oh, nothing. I lost my phone – or I thought I had. I found it in the couch."

"Just now?"

"Yeah. I've been using the one Ken's pilot got me. It doesn't matter." I tossed the Ken-sponsored phone onto the table. It skidded to a halt, bumping into the flowers he'd given her, which were still alive and well. "I tried texting you with the new phone, but you never responded."

Anna looked up, her long eyelashes swooping gracefully. "That was you? Sorry, I was getting an overwhelming number of texts."

"Too popular to answer texts, eh?"

She rolled her eyes. "I didn't think you were coming back, so. Yeah. I didn't think it was you. That's all."

I straightened my posture. "I told you I'd come back. I promised I wouldn't let you suffer through schmoozing on your own."

"We should go, then. I think we're late." She sighed. "I hope the food isn't too adventurous. I've hardly been able to eat all week."

Poor Anna, stuck here with all the rich people food, as she called it. I should've brought her some pierogi.

I held out my arm. "If it is, I'll find something normal for you."

She hesitated before hooking her arm into mine. I stole another glance at her, and she tilted her head ever-so-slightly and smiled.

It hit me square in the chest.

There was no need to come up with a scheme to taunt Ken. Seeing Anna walk in would torture him enough.

• • •

The ballroom did not share the rest of the hotel's modest Swiss design. It looked more like the palace at Versailles, with golden chandeliers, roman columns, twenty-foot archways, and a stained-glass dome in the center of the room. The tables varied from smaller five-seaters to a few longer tables that could fit twenty people. All of them were covered in white and gold silk with white rose displays and towering candles.

The far side of the room housed a small orchestra playing classical music, flanked on both sides by towering sculptures. Around the room, people were sitting and eating, others standing and chatting, drinks in hand.

We were in for it – a standard, boring night.

A waiter greeted us as we walked in, and when he heard Anna's name, rushed her to Ken's personal table.

"Anything you need, Miss," he said, pulling out her seat, "do not hesitate to ask."

Anna thanked him, and as she sat down, a white-gloved waiter appeared, dropping a Lyonnaise salad in front of her.

I took a seat next to her. "No salad for me? I see how it is."

"Why is there an egg on it?" She looked over her shoulder and lowered her voice. "Why is there a *runny* egg on a salad?"

"It's French." I shrugged. "You'll probably like it."

A tiny whimper escaped her, and she stared at it, biting her lip.

"Are you okay?" I asked.

"I'm fine. I just don't think I can eat anything runny."

"Anna!"

We both turned to find the source of the voice. It was a man with a round, firm belly sticking out of his skintight tuxedo. He had no shame, and hadn't even undone the button.

An inspiration, really.

"How are you, my dear?" he asked in a thick accent I couldn't quite identify.

She took a deep breath and smiled. "Very well. How are you?"

"I am always well. It's so good to see young blood at Zermatt. Where's that spicy friend of yours?"

I turned to her. "You made a friend?"

She shot me a look, her smile pressed as though trying not to laugh. "She had to go home early."

"That's too bad," the man said, leaning forward, his eyes lingering on the bust of Anna's dress.

Time to interrupt. "I'm Leo, Anna's fiancé."

He turned, looking me up and down before letting out a guffaw. "Very nice to meet you. More young blood, that's good." He patted himself on the chest. "Join me for a smoke?"

I shook my head. "Anna and I were going to take a look at the sculptures. Please excuse us."

Anna followed my lead, standing from her seat and smiling at him. He walked off, already yelling out a name, accosting another guest.

She grabbed onto my arm. "Thank you."

"You didn't tell me you'd made a friend. Two friends, if you count him." I led us away from the tables and to the perimeter of the room.

"Ha, right. I made one friend, and he followed her around, leering at her."

We reached the first sculpture, a marble sculpture of a man who looked like the wrinkled version of Ken. His father? Was it really a sculpture, or was the old man encased in there?

"What's that guy's story?" I asked.

"He told us his company creates software that protects the will of the people."

I put a hand to my chin. "Which means...what, exactly?"

She lowered her voice and leaned in, the heavenly scent of her perfume filling the space between us. "It allows governments to track people online – everything they say, anything they type. All catalogued and easily searchable."

"Lovely." I let out a sigh. "I'm sure it's a hit in Russia."

"Oh, of course. And everywhere else."

I cocked my head. "Everywhere?"

She nodded. "Depressing, right?"

Another couple approached the sculpture. I stepped out of the way, and Anna followed.

"Who are you supposed to schmooze with, then?" I asked. "Because that guy – yeesh."

"I don't know." She frowned, darting a hand to her stomach. "I don't do well without clear instructions. I made one friend, and that was good, but she wasn't one of these powerful people."

"Were you sent here to make powerful friends?" I asked.

"I don't know why I was sent here. To keep Ken happy, I guess. I'm sure the university thinks he'll throw some money at them."

I smiled. Did Anna really want nothing to do with his money? No wonder she tormented him so.

"Have you been able to eat anything this week?" I asked.

She took her hand off her stomach and shrugged. "Yeah. I'm fine."

"Because I saw an old-fashioned pub in town, and I'm pretty sure they serve burgers and fries."

She looked at me, eyes wide. "Really?"

"We should go. You've clearly made plenty of friends, and what better way to keep Ken's attention than to disappear mysteriously?"

"Mysterious." She laughed. "I talk too much to be mysterious. Sounds nice, though."

"I wouldn't say that."

She stared at me for a moment, then looked back across the ballroom. "I'm supposed to make an impression, I guess. I don't know."

I thought on this for a moment and inspiration struck. I put a hand behind her, sweeping her off her feet and into my arms.

"She's fainted," I yelled out, lifting her into the air. "Out of the way. Someone call a car!"

Anna was too shocked to say anything, her arms clinging to my neck.

Four waiters ran to us, and I rushed past the tables, through the ballroom and the gaping faces, out the door and into the lobby of the hotel.

"Please get us a car, and a coat for her," I demanded.

"Set me *down*," she hissed, and I did as she asked, trying not to grin. A waiter appeared with a black peacoat and wrapped it around her shoulders.

"Your car is waiting, sir," he said, running to open the door.

"Thank you." I turned to Anna, taking her by the hand. "Are you okay to walk?"

Her cheeks were bright pink, her mouth slightly open. "What are you doing?" she whispered.

"Two birds, one stone." I dropped my voice. "You made an impression, and now I'm getting you something to eat."

She laughed, *really* laughed, and had to clap a hand over her mouth.

It got me, too, and I broke into laughter, unable to stop. I put an arm around her as we walked out, laughing like maniacs all the way to the car.

CHAPTER FIFTEEN

Anna

The stunt Leo pulled at the hotel was insane, inappropriate, and exactly what I needed. We were whisked into a waiting car and made it to town just as our laughing fit fizzled out.

Still wearing the stolen coat, I ran into the pub and got a seat at a corner booth. Leo fetched beers for us, and within minutes, the server appeared with a pile of soft pretzels and cheese dip.

A burger, fries, and a side of macaroni and cheese banished the nausea that had been plaguing me for the entirety of the trip.

When we were done eating, I broke the bad news that my mom was throwing an engagement party for us in a month.

"That's good, isn't it? Means she's accepting me?"

I took a sip of beer before answering. "I don't know what it means."

If I hadn't told her the truth, she definitely would *not* be planning an engagement party; she'd be planning Leo's murder.

"Is she big on parties?" he asked.

"She lives for them." That, at least, was true.

I reached out, grabbing one of the remaining pretzels, and used it to scrape the sad remnants of now-hardened cheese from the bowl. "She threw a big engagement party for my sister, so I guess she's just trying to be fair."

"Ah." He finished his beer and set the empty glass down. "The difference being that she liked your sister's fiancé."

I shook my head. "Not really."

"Why not? Was he worse than me?" He leaned in and lowered his voice. "Was he German?"

I laughed. "No. Besides, German is preferrable to Russian."

"What! How?" He made a face. "I'm only *half* Russian."

"Doesn't matter." One more pretzel, then I'd be done. I stuffed it into my mouth and kept talking. "My brother-in-law was mean to my sister on her birthday six years ago, and my mom has never forgiven him for it."

He dropped a fist onto the wooden table with a thud. "She's been mad about that for six years?"

"Yep."

He let out a long breath, puffing out his cheeks. "I'll be so well-behaved that she'll be sad when I'm gone."

When he was gone. When the money would be mine, when the deception would be done, and when Frankie would be free.

It would be wonderful, but all this lying was making my head spin. I finished my beer and flagged the waiter down.

"Two more, please." I turned to look at Leo. "Are you ready to tell me what purpose I'm filling yet?"

He sat back, crossing his arms over his chest. He'd rolled his sleeves up, and his forearms rippled with muscle.

I kept my eyes fixed on my beer.

"I'm almost ready to tell you," he said.

The waiter dropped off the beers and I shoved one toward him. "What does 'almost' mean?"

He uncrossed his arms and pulled the glass closer. "I need to iron out a few details, then I'll tell you everything."

Hopefully my web of lies could make it that long. My mom swore up and down no one else in the family knew about my arrangement with Leo, but when I started asking questions, she quickly unraveled.

"What about Babcia?" I'd asked.

"She doesn't count."

"Mama!"

She sighed. "She figured it out on her own! What was I supposed to do, lie to your grandmother?"

"Yes!" I'd yelled into the phone. "That is *exactly* what you were supposed to do! She's an even bigger blabbermouth than you are!"

"She can hardly hear anymore!"

Not comforting. I ended the conversation soon after.

I looked back at Leo. He was watching me with those intense blue eyes. My breath caught in my throat.

What was it about his stare? It felt like I had his complete focus, like he was recording every detail. Had to be an artist thing.

I raised my glass. "To our love."

"Our love," he said with a laugh.

• • •

We flew back to Madison the next morning. As we were about to get onto the plane, Ken flagged me down.

"Go ahead," I told Leo. "I'll catch up."

He cast one look at Ken before getting onto the plane, joking with the pilot, whom he'd apparently befriended.

Ken was breathless. "I didn't get a chance to see you last night."

That wasn't true. I'd spotted him staring at me when we came in, and every time I looked up, I caught him looking away.

There was no need to make it awkward, though. "I know, I'm sorry. I wasn't feeling well."

He looked up at me, his forehead creased, his eyes full of concern. "I hope you're feeling better?"

"Yes, much better." I'd had trouble falling asleep the night before because I was so stuffed from all the pretzels and beer, but again, best to keep that charming tidbit to myself. "Thank you for everything. It was wonderful."

He nodded, opening his mouth to say something, then stopped himself.

I waited, and after a moment, he spoke again. "I know this isn't my place, but..." He looked over his shoulder, then back at me. "Do you know what Leo was doing in Poland?"

Here we go. "Just some business, I'm not sure. Why?"

"I'm afraid – well, he may be hiding something from you."

Ya think?

I took a deep breath. "He's mysterious. Artists. You know how they are."

He nodded. "Of course."

"I'll talk to him."

"Sure." He flashed me a strained, brief sort of smile. "Safe travels, and don't be a stranger."

I got on the plane and tried to block the conversation from my mind, which went about as well as can be expected.

I spent the flight working on my laptop and peering at Leo across from me. I kept imagining scenarios where he was involved with the Polish mafia (if there was such a thing), Russian smugglers, or perhaps both, with a looming war in the near future.

Would I get caught up in it, and would it result in my kidnapping? At least if that happened, my stalker would know where to find me. He probably even had the resources to rescue me, a distinct benefit of having a billionaire stalker.

Until now, I'd been unprotected. Once, after watching the movie *Taken,* Lisa asked my dad what would happen if she were "taken."

My dad clasped his hands together, and after an impressive twenty seconds of pretending to think, said, "You would probably die."

She did not appreciate his honesty, or our hysterical laughter at her indignation.

The flight home was peaceful, thankfully, and undisturbed by mafia-smuggler-sky pirates. When we landed, Leo and I went our separate ways.

At least, we did at first. Part of our ploy was convincing people we were actually in love. It meant lunches shared on university benches, visits to my parents, and even a trip to the ballet. (Leo insisted. I told him he was showing his Russian side, and he needed to find the Polish side if he was going to survive. He responded to this by inviting me to his office and forcing piles of food onto me. Touché.)

After failing to come up with an excuse as to why we couldn't attend the engagement party, I found myself driving Leo to the Polish club that dreaded Saturday evening.

"What's a Polish club?" Leo asked.

"It's a magical place with drop ceilings and wood paneling where all the local Poles go to eat kielbasa, dance to Disco Polo, and drink vodka."

"Sounds fun. Can I become a member?"

I made the turn into the parking lot, mortified to see there were only three spots left. "No."

"Why not?"

"Because you'd get destroyed in the pierogi eating contest."

His eyes widened. "There's a pierogi eating contest?"

I parked and turned off the van. "No."

That was a lie. There was an annual pierogi eating contest, but he wouldn't be around for it.

"Too bad. I could've been a real star," he said wistfully. "Speaking of stars, how'd the meeting go with Frankie's star lawyer?"

"Good, actually. He seems nice and sleazy."

Leo paused. "That's a good thing?"

"For a defense lawyer? Yeah."

We got out of the van and Leo turned to me. "How do I look?"

He'd worn a suit, as I'd requested, but he'd managed to mess it up. I thought he'd wear something black, something boring, so I could shove him in the corner and keep him away from my relatives.

But no, he had to show up in a muted jade velvet suit, looking like he'd walked out of a Rolex ad, his blue eyes even more piercing. He was *far* too handsome to escape harassment from the aunts and ridicule from the cousins.

"Just...listen." I stopped, picking a bit of floof off his shoulder. "Don't talk to anyone."

He laughed. "What?"

"Just..." I waved a hand. "Don't. You'll live longer."

Leo frowned. "I'll do my best."

I started walking, then immediately stopped. "Also, if my mom wore her flying squirrel coat, and my dad is making fun of her, don't join in."

"Flying squirrel coat?"

"It's got fur on the arms and it's all wide and – you'll know it when you see it. Don't say anything, don't encourage him."

"Got it."

We turned toward the building as the front door burst open and my Babcia stomped outside.

"Zuzia! *You lost weight,*" she yelled in Polish. "*Beautiful!*"

"*Thank you, Babcia,*" I said, grabbing Leo by the hand and pulling him forward.

"*Is that him?*" She smiled at Leo and waved. "*The fake husband?*"

I shut my eyes. I should've never gotten out of the van.

CHAPTER SIXTEEN

Leo

A second woman stepped outside, grabbing the older lady by the forearm and yelling at her in Polish.

I stood there, waving back like a dope.

"I said don't talk to anyone," Anna hissed, pulling my arm down.

"She waved first!" I watched the two women as they wrestled with the door. "Who is that?"

"That's my grandma, my Babcia," Anna said. "She's not all there. Don't take anything she says seriously."

Anna started walking toward the battling women and I followed. "Does she speak English?"

"No." Anna paused, pulling a lip gloss from her purse. "Not that she can't speak English. She just doesn't."

"Ah." Whatever she'd said, it sounded like she was excited to see me.

When we got to the building, they stopped struggling with one another and turned their attention onto us.

"Zuzia!" Babcia yelled out, putting her arms up and planting a kiss on each of Anna's cheeks.

"*Cześć*, Babcia," she said.

"It's so nice to meet you," the other woman said, beaming at me. "I'm Ela."

"Very nice to meet you. I'm Leo."

"I know." She let out a little squeal and looked at Anna. "He's so handsome! Where did you find him?"

"He was on sale at Marshall's," Anna said. "Let's go inside, Ciocia."

"Ciocia means aunt, right?" I asked.

Ela grabbed my face with both hands. "That's right, Leo, and now I will be your ciocia, too."

She kissed both of my cheeks, then pulled the door open, calling out, "Come, come, we have a table for you!"

Babcia led the way, and Ciocia Ela followed. I looked at Anna with the intent of winking at her, but her stare was fixed straight ahead, her jaw clenched.

Better to save the jokes for later. Anna wasn't in the mood for any of that now. For some reason, lying to her entire family was making her tense.

We walked into the front room, a dimly lit space lined with couches and a coat rack. The walls were dark wood paneling, and Anna hung up her coat before pressing on. Her grandma and aunt bickered in Polish ahead of us, but Anna was silent.

We walked around a corner and into a much larger room. The wood paneling was partially covered with white curtains and multi-colored Christmas lights on one wall. Another was coated with panel after panel of silver tinsel foil fringe.

The tables were decked out with white tablecloths and platters overflowing with dried meats, sausages, stuffed peppers, pierogi, and bread rolls. Chairs wrapped in shining organza, with red bows tied at the backs, crowded every space, and for a moment, I wondered if this was an impromptu wedding.

That would be awkward. There were enough guests for it. How many people were in here? A hundred? Two?

The space was entirely carpeted except for the far side of the room, which housed a hardwood dance floor next to a raised stage. There was a live band blasting a lively tune, all four members in matching sequined shirts, and a shining disco ball overhead.

"Is that an accordion?" I asked Anna, nodding toward the stage.

Her response was drowned out by a chorus of voices. "He's here! He's here!"

Within seconds, we were surrounded. They pulled me forward, then to the side, then the other, a hoard of older women kissing my cheeks and petting my hair.

"Hi, *cześć*," I repeated through laughter. Something thudded onto my shoe, and I looked down to see a little girl, maybe three years old, in a poofy pink dress.

Anna stooped down and picked her up. "What are *you* doing here?"

She blew a raspberry, and the girl giggled and screeched before pulling away and saying, "Again!"

Three women talked to me at once – two in English, one in Polish – and finally, apparently frustrated, one took me by the hand and pulled me toward a table.

There were at least ten guys already sitting there, eating and drinking, and I was plopped into a chair in the center.

Anna's dad Stanley was in the seat directly across from me. "Leo, you made it."

A woman speaking at me in rapid Polish shoved a loaded plate into my hands.

I thanked her and set it down. "I did."

Anna was across the room with her mom. I waved, receiving an identical stony look from both of them.

"If you need it," Stanley said, "there's a window in the bathroom you can jump out of."

He laughed, as did the guy next to him.

I smiled. "Thanks. I'll keep it in mind."

It was easier than expected to avoid speaking to Anna's family. First I was plied with delicious food, then a stupendously drunk uncle put his arm around me and spit a story into my face for half an hour.

Ciocia Ela sought me out as well, mostly leading the conversation.

"I saw the new Bon Johns movie," she said.

I had to think for a moment. "You mean James Bond?"

"Yes, James Bond. It was a lot of fighting and running. *I Don't Want to Die*, I think it was called."

"Oh..." My wheels were turning. "*No Time to Die?*"

Her eyes brightened. "You saw it too?"

"No, but did you like it?"

She shrugged. "Not really."

I waited to see what else she was going to say, or why she brought it up, but instead she just cupped my face in her hand and told me she would bring me something to eat.

Stanley, who was in an argument about how to properly care for newly laid sod, waved a hand at me.

"Leo, were you listening?"

I shook my head. "Sorry, no."

"If the grass ever dries," he said, pointing a finger at me, "you are a failure. Remember that."

He went on about this for twenty minutes, and I took the chance to finish a second plate of food – gołąbki, or stuffed cabbages, just as my mom made them, and pizza pierogi, unlike anything my mom had ever made.

I was still stuffing my face when Stanley turned his attention back on me. "Now Leo," he said, narrowing his eyes, "what is your favorite Dostoyevsky book? *Crime and Punishment*?"

This was embarrassing. I'd never read Dostoyevsky. Apparently, I only read romance novels, and that was to impress women.

More embarrassingly, it never worked.

I sat back, crossing my arms. "It's hard to say."

"Do you prefer English or the original Russian?"

I scratched the back of my neck, pretending to think, and in that moment, a wonderful and horrible thing happened. One of Anna's teenage cousins tapped me on the shoulder and asked if I knew how to dance.

"I don't, sorry." I was less embarrassed of this than of my illiteracy, but still embarrassed nevertheless.

She grinned, displaying her silver and pink braces. "I can teach you!"

I looked over my shoulder for Anna. She was already on the dance floor, spinning around wildly and laughing.

"That's okay. I have terrible rhythm."

"Come on. Don't be a baby!"

I shook my head. "No, really, I'm too full."

"Leo, are you afraid of a little dancing?" Stanley yelled, and the table erupted into laughter.

I clasped my hands in front of me. They could make fun of me, they could taunt me, but I was not going to get onto that dance floor and do anything that resembled dancing.

The song ended, and Anna, spotting this scuffle from across the room, made her way over to us.

"Is there a problem?" she asked.

There was a slight sheen to her forehead and her cheeks were flushed pink. Everyone here had to think she was glowing from her new love affair; she sold it well enough, looking perfect – always so perfect.

"Your boyfriend is afraid to dance with me," the girl complained.

Anna smiled. "He doesn't know how. I have to show him."

Another accordion-heavy song began and Anna wrapped both of her hands around my wrist.

What was the use in fighting? I stood and let her drag me to the dance floor.

"Put one hand on my waist," she commanded.

With all eyes on us, I didn't dare let my hand dip too low. "Okay."

"Now try to feel the beat. One, two, three. One, two, three."

I tried to follow her. "And bounce? Like this?"

"A little less like you're Frankenstein's monster taking his first steps, but yes."

A laugh burst out of me and I released the stiffness from my shoulders. "I'm sorry. I'm not good at this."

"You're not," she said, a smile on her lips, "but I appreciate you trying."

It was the first time I'd seen her smile that day. I pressed on, trying to move to the music. "Your family's really nice."

"They're really *something*," she said, lifting my arm up and spinning herself beneath it.

When she stopped, I pulled her back in. "I like them."

"Maybe it's time for you to tell me about your family?" she asked, drawing closer.

I looked into her eyes and my heart squeezed in my chest. It was in that moment I realized something: I couldn't tell her no.

It was not the same situation as her Babcia, who could speak English, but chose not to. I was *incapable* of telling her no. I was going to tell her everything, every secret, every heartbreak.

This was a dangerous place I'd never planned to be.

"Okay," I said, breathless from the activity, or maybe from how close she was. "Tomorrow."

"Tomorrow?" She stopped moving, dropping her hands to her sides. "Really?"

I nodded. "Come to my house. I'll tell you everything you want to know."

She smiled, pleased with herself. "Good. Now give me your other hand and I'll show you a double twist."

CHAPTER SEVENTEEN

Anna

We made it two songs before Lisa cut in and demanded her turn with Leo.

"You're just like Noah and what's-her-face in *The Notebook*," she said, pulling him by the hand.

"Her name was Allie," Leo said.

"How did you know that?" I asked him.

He shrugged, grinning, and I rolled my eyes. "How are we anything like that toxic love story?"

"You know." She lowered her voice. "The part where the mom tries to sabotage them."

Leo leaned in. "I can still hear you."

"Allie's mom was right," I said. "Noah was emotionally manipulative and obsessive. The other guy was much better."

"Is that what your mom thinks of me?" Leo asked. "What does she call him in the movie? 'Trash, trash! Not for you'?"

I stared at him. Why did he have an encyclopedia of romance stories in his head?

"No, of course not," Lisa rushed to say. "She just might, I don't know, have some tricks left. I don't know! Don't ask me! I don't know!"

Poor Lisa. She truly didn't know what was going on, and she was going to flip out when I told her the truth. "I'm not worried." I said. "Enjoy your dance, and watch your toes."

Dancing is a lot of fun, but it's sort of like a child's birthday party. If you invite one person in the class, you have to invite them all, and by the time I accepted a dance from every uncle and cousin in this place, my mom could be on a megaphone announcing all of my secrets.

I needed to keep an eye on her. After scanning the crowd, I spotted her huddled in a corner with my sister Sarah, their backs turned to the rest of the room.

Not good. I made my way over.

"Hey Mama," I said slowly, putting a hand on her shoulder, "what are you guys talking about?"

She turned to me, eyes wide, and shook her head. "Nothing." Then she paused. "Nothing bad."

"Ah." I took a seat at the table. Heat pulsed from my skin.

"Are you hot? Do you need a drink?" my mom asked, jumping to her feet.

"No, I'm fine."

She shook her head. "Diet Coke? I'll get you a Diet Coke."

There was no stopping her—she was already halfway to the bar.

Sarah sat back, her arms and legs crossed. I turned to her, but she avoided my gaze, instead staring straight ahead.

"Thanks for coming," I said.

"Thanks for telling me you were getting married."

There it was. The disdain I deserved.

I moved into the seat next to her. "I'm sorry, I tried calling, but things have been crazy. I meant to—"

Her head snapped in my direction. "Do you know we had to cancel our trip to the indoor waterpark to come to this? Marley cried for two *hours*."

The familiar sinking feeling hit my chest and I shrank down. "I'm sorry. You didn't have to come, Mama just decided to do this and…"

"Of course we had to come! You've been anti-marriage all your life and now I find out you've made some pact and changed your mind? I thought you were having a psychotic break. I had to see for myself."

"I'm not having a psychotic break." I shifted in my seat, trying to get closer to her. "It's complicated. I wish I could tell you everything, but I can't. Not yet."

She rolled her eyes. "Yeah, okay. Like anyone ever tells me anything."

"I'm really sorry you canceled the trip and Marley was upset," I said. "If I had known…"

Sarah cut me off. "Save it, Anna." She got up and walked away.

I stood to go after her when a high-pitched scream caught my ear.

I stopped, turning to look for the source. It came from the bar – my mom!

"Mama," I called out, rushing over. "What's wrong?"

Still holding a cup in each hand, she pointed down the hallway and whispered, "The police are here."

"What?" I looked, squinting, as a man in a green uniform stepped into view.

He looked at us and my mom screamed again, longer this time. The band stopped playing, and a general confusion settled on the crowd.

"They're here for Frankie," she said, her voice shaking as she dropped both drinks onto the floor with a splash.

It took all my force to pull her into a chair. "Stop yelling. You don't know that."

I looked over my shoulder just as my dad and Frankie disappeared into the men's room.

The old out-the-window trick. I'd used it many times, like when my dad and I spent a New Year's stealing people's cell phones and hiding them in the ceiling. Once they figured out what we'd done, we had to make a quick exit.

Leave it to my dad to be cool under pressure. As much chill as my mom didn't have, my dad more than made up for it, which helped when she pointed and screamed at things, as she was doing at that moment.

"Frankie just left with Tata," I said in a whisper. "It's fine. Don't say anything. I'll do the talking, okay?"

All the color had left her face. "Okay."

The boos of several inebriated uncles carried across the dance floor as the officer made his way into the dining hall.

I fixed a polite smile on my face and approached him. He looked stern, particularly with his tactical vest and large mustache, but he gave me a smile-frown before nodding and stepping aside.

A woman in a matching uniform strode out from behind him. I recognized her, but my brain wasn't able to process the information, forcing me to stare at the CBP on her chest.

As usual, my mouth took over before my brain could catch up. "Nikki?" I walked toward her. "Nikki Crouch?"

"*Officer* Crouch." She raised her chin, looking down at me with the pucker-lip face I'd nearly forgotten.

Her skin was unwrinkled, her brown hair shorter, but the same straight style, and she was just as thin as when she'd gotten our tenth-grade gym class to nickname me "Thunder Thigh Anna."

(My thighs thundered on, and you know what? Old Thunder Thigh Anna could hop, skip, and obfuscate her way around a bully these days).

Leo appeared at my side, loudly whispering, "That's not your nemesis Nikki, is it?"

I nodded, keeping my eyes on her. She was standing with her hands on her hips, saying something to her partner.

Leo spoke again. "You didn't tell me she was a cop."

I pulled away, startled by his hoarse voice in my ear. Why was he so bad at whispering?

"I'm a Border Patrol *Federal* Agent." She pointed a finger at the letters on her chest and flashed a smile. "We got a complaint about an illegal alien hiding in this club."

"Uh." I looked over my shoulder. There was a trio of uncles whose booing had morphed full-blown heckling.

Thankfully, it was in Polish and she wouldn't be able to understand the impressively creative names they were calling her.

"What are you looking at? You got something to tell me?" Nikki said, staring down Ciocia Ela.

Ciocia Ela took one look at Nikki, laughed, and walked away. A small group followed her lead, and as the tension broke, a gaggle of children ran squealing to the dance floor, delighted to find it empty.

"No aliens here, Nikki," I said with a shrug. "Thanks for checking in, though."

She smirked. "You think this is a joke?"

An *overwhelming* number of inappropriate responses came to my mind, and in my struggle not to say them out loud, I fell silent.

Leo managed to come up with an appropriate answer. "No, officer, we take this very seriously."

She looked him up and down. "Are you the fiancé?" When she saw my narrowed eyes, she added, "I saw the announcement in the paper."

The paper.

My mom had to go and announce our engagement in the paper. All part of her brilliant plan, which she didn't feel the need to tell me about, which of course lured my nemesis here, because why wouldn't it?

I shot my mom a look, but she was still in a catatonic freeze, sitting in a chair with Sarah at her side.

"I am. Nice to meet you," Leo said, offering a handshake.

She recoiled, looking down at his hand as though it was covered in scabies. She turned to me. "You're a little old for a big wedding, don't you think?"

Oh, dear Nikki. Not only had she managed to not age, she managed to not mature, either. She was still the same petty, jealous, nasty girl I'd known all those years ago.

Which meant I still knew how to push her buttons.

I shot Leo, my objectively hot fiancé, an adoring look. "You're never too old for love."

Lisa, who had been quietly watching from the sidelines, stepped toward us with fury on her face. "I don't see a ring on *your* finger, Nikki."

"All right," the male officer said, his hands up. "Why don't we all—"

Nikki cut him off. "Give me your phone, Lisa."

Lisa took a step back. "Ew, no."

"I'm conducting a search," Nikki said in a bright tone, a broad smile spanning her face. "That's an order. Hand it over."

Lisa crossed her arms. "I'm an attorney. I know my rights. You can get a warrant."

"Actually," Leo said in a low voice, "border patrol doesn't need a warrant to search your phone. They can just take it."

"We're not at the border!" Lisa said, throwing her hands to her sides.

Leo cleared his voice. "Technically, anything within a hundred miles of the border counts as the border."

Why did Leo know so much about border patrol? Was he the illegal alien they were looking for?

More importantly, did he know about the escape window?

"You should listen to your Russian brother-in-law," Nikki said to Lisa in a syrupy-sweet voice.

Lisa responded in a mockingly high-pitched voice. "Except we're five hundred miles from Canada, Officer *Crotch*."

Oh good. Lisa had decided to revive Nikki's high school nickname. This was going swimmingly.

I took a step and pushed Lisa back. "How about we all—"

"You're eighty miles from Lake Michigan," Nikki snapped, sticking out her hand. "That counts, Miss Lawyer. So *give it!*"

Lisa bounced forward and spat a laugh into her face. "Ha! Joke's on you. I lost my phone yesterday, so if you find it, you'll be doing me a favor."

"Oh really? If you don't produce it, I'll have to arrest you."

Nikki's partner and I stepped in at the same time.

He said, "Let's bring this down a notch," as I said, "She definitely doesn't have her phone."

I gave Lisa a stern look and she rolled her eyes before retreating.

Nikki had already moved on, cupping her hands around her mouth like a megaphone. "Someone needs to turn on the lights."

My cousin Vito stopped in his tracks. "Lights? We have lights here?"

His dad called from the other side of the room. "Anyone see lights?"

"No lights!" Babcia yelled, then added in Polish, *"Turn off the lights so I don't have to see this ugly duckling anymore."*

Nikki was undeterred. She straightened her posture and yelled, "All right, everyone, line up in front of me. I'm going to need to see proof of citizenship. Passports, identification. Move it."

I sighed, shooting a pleading glance to the normal-seeming officer. "We don't have our passports. We're in the middle of Wisconsin."

Nikki took a step toward me and lowered her voice. "Anna, if you keep getting in the way of me doing my job, you won't like what happens."

Leo held up a finger. "American citizens aren't required to show proof of citizenship upon request."

She spun around. "Oh yeah, tough guy? Why don't you go back to Russia?"

"I'm an America citizen," he said, his tone even and friendly, "and I'll be staying here."

Nikki's partner, literally wringing his hands together, whispered something in her ear.

"I can't hear you," she barked.

"Maybe we should come back later," he said, loud enough for all of us to hear.

"Go wait in the car," she muttered, turning back to face the room. "Line starts here, people."

As I could have predicted, my relatives did not line up to show their papers, and instead wandered off to get shots of liquor, load plates with food, and successfully heckle the band back onstage.

Even my mother and her frayed nerves were nowhere to be seen.

"Single file!" Nikki called out.

Her partner put his arm up, half-heartedly waving people over, just as the wheezy notes of an accordion rang out.

I stifled a laugh.

Nikki spun around, glaring knives at me. "You're not doing yourself any favors."

Thirty years old and still acting like a child. Nikki had always been power-hungry, and at first, realizing she had a job with actual power had sent a jolt of terror through my body, almost awakening my nervous stomach monster for an emergency meeting.

Now, however... "Officer Crouch, I'm first in line and awaiting your orders."

"Me too," Leo said, buttoning his jacket, again looking like the newest addition to the Bond franchise.

My eyes lingered for a moment too long. I forced myself to turn back to Nikki, who was furiously talking to her partner.

He was distracted, looking over her head, his mouth hanging open. She stood on her tiptoes, trying to see what he was looking at. "What is it?"

"That's Ken Fielding!" he said, shouting over the music. "I can't believe it!"

My stomach sank. I might need that emergency meeting after all, realizing *that* was what Lisa meant when she said my mom still had some tricks left.

Ken strolled over, an easy smile on his face and an absolutely enormous bottle of champagne in his hands. "Hello, officers." He nodded at me. "Anna. Leo."

As always, he was impeccably dressed, and he smelled fresh and rich. He set the champagne on a nearby table.

Leo shook his hand. "Ken. Fancy meeting you here."

Nikki sighed a "hello," and her partner finally found his voice. "Mr. Fielding, I never thought – I'm a huge fan – we talk about you all the time, my brother and I – we have an investment club, and it's an honor to meet you. You're – "

Ken grabbed his hand for a vigorous handshake. "No, it's an honor to meet you."

He grinned, clasping his hand with both hands. "Wow. Thank you."

My mother, the tricky minx, appeared out of nowhere. The color had returned to her cheeks, and her lipstick was fresh and shining. "Ken, you're here!"

He took her by both hands as she delicately kissed his cheeks.

He handed her the bottle of champagne. "Mrs. Makowski, thank you for the invitation."

"I'm so glad you could come. Isn't this nice, Zuzia?"

I looked at her, but before I could open my mouth, she grabbed my wrist and murmured, "Be polite to your guests."

She then walked off, taking the champagne with her.

Ken was oblivious to the high-stakes operation Nikki was trying to kick off. "The music is fantastic! Are they singing in Polish?"

"Yeah. Anna's dad wrote this one," Leo said. "It's about a boy who lost his finger in a tractor accident."

Ken frowned. "Really? It sounds so upbeat."

"It's a love letter to the finger," Leo explained, avoiding my glare.

"I guess I have no choice but to get on the mic so people can hear me," Nikki announced, but her partner took a break from staring adoringly at Ken to grab her arm.

"Wait," he said. "I think we're okay."

Ken slapped a hand to his shoulder. "Oh, is there a problem?"

"No, not at all," he said. "It's really nothing. Just checking in."

Nikki's mouth popped open, but even she remained quiet.

"Are you staying for the party?" Ken asked.

He laughed far too loudly. "No, sir. We were just leaving, but we're always at your service. I love your planes, by the way. I always talk about your planes."

"He does," Nikki said, her tone flat.

Ken pulled a card from his pocket. "How about you give my assistant a call and we get you on a tour?"

He grabbed the card, his mouth open, his head vigorously nodding. "That would be amazing."

Nikki grabbed him with one hand and pointed at me with the other. "Don't think you've gotten away with anything."

I nodded. "Nice seeing you again."

We watched as they walked out and disappeared around a corner.

"I didn't mean to intrude," Ken said. "Your mom was extremely persistent about me coming to this party."

"No, please," I shook my head. "We're happy to have you. And you were a huge help just now, so thank you."

"Nothing we couldn't handle on our own, though," Leo said, putting an arm around me.

I shot him a side glance, but he kept his eyes on Ken.

Had everyone lost their minds? Did Leo *actually* feel threatened by Ken? And what was with my mom luring Ken to the party in the first place?

Lisa swooped in, a wide smile on her face. "Hi Ken. It's nice to finally meet you. I'm Lisa."

Huh. She seemed unusually comfortable with meeting a pseudo-celebrity. Almost like she knew he was coming.

I glared at her. "Lisa, when you were talking about *The Notebook*, did you—"

She cut me off. "Can I get you a drink, Ken?"

"That would be lovely," he said, flashing his dazzling smile.

Coward. Lisa was always a coward, the family peacekeeper, and I found it especially annoying in that moment.

Why hadn't she warned me! I could've run away, through the window with my dad and Frankie.

"Excuse me," I said, clearing my throat. "I need to check on something with my mom."

I broke free of Leo's embrace and shot him a look. He smiled, then turned to follow Ken and Lisa to the bar.

Dancing couples had spilled off the packed dance floor and into the aisles. I wove through, skirting my way around the perimeter, pressing against the tables that had been pushed against the walls.

I found my mom in the kitchen, oohing and aahing over the giant bottle of champagne with her two sisters.

"Look at this!" she said, holding it up. "It's half the size of Babcia!"

I crossed my arms. "What's he doing here, Mama?"

Her smile faded, and she set the bottle down. She nodded at her sisters, and they left, giggling, through the swinging kitchen door.

"Frankie and Tata got home safely," she said evenly.

"I didn't think they were in any danger, but that's good." I raised my eyebrows. "I'm pretty sure you're the reason Nikki came here."

"Me? I don't talk to Nikki! I stopped cleaning her mom's house years ago. You know she still lives there with them?"

I didn't know, but now was not the time to get tricked into gossiping with her. "She saw your newspaper announcement and decided to come here for a power trip."

My mom shook her head. "She's always been jealous of you. Jealous, jealous, jealous."

"Why did you do it? And why did you invite Ken?"

She let out a breath and rested her hands on the counter between us. "Zuzia, I think you forget."

I put my hands on my hips. "Forget what?"

"That you are not really engaged."

I looked over my shoulder, my eyes bulging from their sockets. "*Sh!*"

"What? I think you are starting to lose your sense. Just because Leo is a looker doesn't mean you should ignore Ken."

"Since when – why would I – " I stopped, regaining my train of thought. "I'm not marrying either of them."

She stared at me for a moment before picking up the champagne bottle and handing it to me. "Just remember, one day he will be gone, and then what?"

The bottle was obnoxiously large, and the label was in French. I didn't speak French. I hated how heavy it was; I hated everything about it.

I put the bottle on the table. "And then nothing. We'll all move on with our lives."

I walked out, leaving the champagne behind.

CHAPTER EIGHTEEN

Leo

After the commotion, the mood changed. The revelers went in one direction, growing increasingly and boisterously drunk, and Anna went in another. Her smiles became brief, her gaze lingered aimlessly, and perhaps worst of all, it felt like she was avoiding me.

I tried telling myself it was because of Nikki, but I feared it was due to someone else – the charming Mr. Fielding.

When Anna was off dancing, he walked up to me. "Leo. I hear Kraków is beautiful in the fall."

He was trying to make me flinch. It wouldn't work. "It is. I'm surprised to see you here."

He smiled. "Same to you."

Absolutely shameless. I nodded my head to him and walked away.

Inviting Anna to Zermatt was one thing, but showing up at our engagement party with an obvious obsession with the bride-to-be?

It was beyond crass. He was a vulgar and ostentatious man, and he only got away with it because he owned a company that made cool planes.

I was sitting at a table, watching Ken and Anna on the other side of the room, when Ciocia Ela slipped into the seat next to me.

"He's the rich guy, isn't he?"

I nodded. "A friend."

"Your friend?" A grin spread across her face. "Or Anna's?"

We both turned to look at them. Ken was laughing and touching Anna on the shoulder.

I turned away. "More Anna's friend, I would say."

What use was jealousy? I knew Anna couldn't resist Ken's charms forever. Before long, they'd ride off into the sunset on one of his ever-present jets, leaving me behind.

Everyone left in the end. I'd lived it enough times to know Anna would be no different.

Ela picked up a fork and tapped it on her champagne glass. "Anna has enough friends."

The clinking echoed, multiplying as the guests picked up their own glasses and started to cheer.

I caught Anna's eye from across the room and she smiled, a redness rushing to her cheeks.

"Go," Ela said, pushing me to stand. "You have to kiss! It's the rule!"

I knew it was better not to get attached in the first place, but apparently, I needed to learn it one more time. And who was I to challenge the rules?

I stood from my seat and jogged over to Anna, taking her by the hands.

"Your aunt said we had to."

She laughed. "By all means."

It was hard not to laugh along with her. I put my hand on her cheek and closed my eyes. In that split second, I felt her lips against mine, soft, slightly parted, and I completely lost my breath.

Cheers erupted all around us and I opened my eyes, breaking away.

Anna waved a hand at the boisterous crowd. "Okay, okay!"

She looked up at me and smiled, a real smile this time, and I reminded myself to breathe.

An uncle emerged from the kitchen with two-gallon bottles of vodka under each arm, and we made the joint decision to take our leave. According to Anna, "Nothing good happens after the vodka bottles with pumps appear."

The first few minutes of the drive home were quiet. I wanted to talk about Ken without looking jealous, but couldn't figure out how before Anna's questioning started.

"What's with your extensive knowledge of the Border Patrol?"

I cleared my throat. "I lived in the US as a refugee until I was twenty-one."

"A refugee?" She shot me side eye. "Are you making this up?"

"No." I stole a glance at her. The curls in her hair had loosened, somehow only looking more elegant. Some of the glitter in her eyeshadow had fallen onto her cheeks, catching the moonlight. "Come over. I'll tell you everything."

She bit her lip. "When?"

"Right now, tomorrow. Monday. I don't care." The paperwork wasn't all in place, but she deserved to know what was going on. I had the feeling Ken might be watching me, and I didn't trust what sort of nonsense he'd tell her in his brazen courtship.

Anna pulled into my driveway and put the van into park. "Let's do tomorrow."

"Tomorrow is perfect." I opened my car door. It would be so easy to lean over and kiss her again...

"I'll see you then."

"Goodnight."

. . .

Anna arrived the next morning promptly at ten.

I heard her van sputter into the driveway and opened the door as she walked up. "I hope you have room for breakfast."

She winced. "I already ate."

"I made blueberry-mascarpone French toast."

"Well, there's always room for brunch," she said, walking up the sidewalk.

I grinned. Anna was never one to turn down food. So many of my friends back in New York didn't eat carbs, or didn't eat after noon, or only ate when the moon was in Virgo.

Anna was too fun for that, and maybe just lucky – she was stunning, and probably didn't have to worry about what she ate at all.

She followed me past the living room and into the kitchen. I'd set our places at the kitchen island, as I'd failed to buy a kitchen table despite it being on my to-do list for the past few weeks.

Anna noticed. "What's up with you not having any furniture? Are you sure you live here?"

I pulled out a seat for her. "I do. I even passed the home visit."

"Home visit for what?"

I turned and picked up a spatula for the French toast, almost dropping it. My hands were cold and a little shaky. "It's a long story. Do you want to eat first?"

"Can you eat and talk?"

I had no appetite. "Sure."

I served her two slices to start, topped with blueberries and a dusting of powdered sugar.

"This looks so good!" She picked up her fork and took a bite. "Yeah. Even better than it looks. Thank you so much."

"You're welcome." I took a seat next to her, pulling a photo album off the seat next to me. "I've got some things to show you."

"Okay." She leaned over, still chewing.

At least one of us was relaxed. I opened to the first page. "That's my mom when she came to the US. She was twenty-nine, and I was six."

"She's so pretty." Anna leaned in. "Where's your dad?"

"He didn't make it."

She looked at me with wide eyes, and I corrected myself. "I mean, he didn't make it with us then. I told you he'd been arrested? For criticizing the government."

"Oh, right. Yeah."

"He was – he *is* – a celebrated mathematician. He thought it would protect him from being arrested. It didn't." I flipped the page.

"So you and your mom were just...alone?"

I nodded. "After my dad was arrested, she was scared. Terrified, really. She managed to escape the Soviet Union because she had an uncle who was high in the communist party. Came to the US with practically nothing."

"Where did you go?"

"Utica, in upstate New York. Her mom had a friend there from Poland. They took us in, got her work at a butcher shop, a place called Pulaski's Meat Market."

Anna ran a finger along the page, the faces smiling back at us in faded colors.

I went on. "My mom had studied math in Poland, but she didn't finish her degree. It was worthless here anyway."

"Sounds like my mom." Anna looked up at me. "She made it work, though?"

"Somehow, she did. We had help, too." I smiled. "When I was eight, I needed to get my tonsils taken out, but we didn't have insurance or the money to do it. As the story goes, a Jewish doctor took my case for free."

"Why?"

"Because she heard my mom was Polish, and during the war, some Poles hid her family members from the Nazis."

Anna let out a breath. "Wow."

I flipped the page. "My dad got out of prison after five years, and a bunch of academics schemed to get him to the US. That's him when he arrived."

She leaned down, studying the picture. "Aw. What a happy family."

"Sort of." I took a breath, steadying myself. "We were missing my brother, Dima."

"Was he in prison, too?"

I shook my head. "Dima was ten years older than me. He'd gotten in with a group back home – sort of a gang. Organized crime, disorganized crime. Whatever you call it, he was making money and wouldn't leave. My mom had to make a choice – leave him behind, or risk going to prison herself and losing me completely."

Her eyes were wide and misted with tears. "That's awful."

I stared at the picture of the three of us. We were happy then, happy to be reunited, happy to be safe, but it had always been overshadowed by Dima.

On the same page was a picture Dima had sent us around that time. He was wearing a leather jacket, sitting behind the wheel of a new car.

"It's complicated. He said he was doing what he had to do. He sent us money; he made sure I had enough for art lessons and supplies." I closed the album and pulled out my phone.

"He never wanted to leave. Not until recently. This is a picture of him from last year."

Anna grabbed the phone and pulled it close. "Oh my gosh! Who is this *heavily* pregnant lady?"

"His wife, Agnieszka." I smiled at her. "Polish, as you might guess."

"The men in your family seem to have a type."

My chest felt heavy, but I laughed. "We might."

I took the phone back. There were too many pictures of Dima and Agnieszka. I flipped through, keeping my eyes focused, or trying to as tears clouded my vision. Somehow, this was even harder than I'd expected.

"They were trying to move. Building a house near Kraków, actually. They almost made it." I handed the phone over to her before turning and pouring a mug of coffee. It burned, but it was helping the tightness in my throat. "That's Oliver. Dima's son."

She squealed. "Leo, he's adorable!" She looked at me, then back at the picture. "He looks *just* like you."

"I know." The warmth from the mug spread to my hands. "Do you want some coffee?"

"No thanks."

I took a swig, turning to face her, my voice steady again. "They were driving a moving truck from Moscow when Dima and Agnieszka were killed in a traffic accident."

Anna gasped. "Leo. I'm so sorry."

I met her eyes. There were tears brimming at the edges, and I had to look away.

"It was eight months ago. Oliver has been with Agnieszka's aunt in Poland."

A silence hung between us.

I set the mug down. Did she understand why I'd waited so long to tell her? Did she think I was crazy?

Most importantly, would she still help when I told her what I needed her to do?

Anna set my phone on the counter and looked up at me. "I love him. Do you have any more pictures?"

Air rushed back into my lungs and the tingling in my fingers started to resolve. "Of course. I have thousands. I'll be right back."

I ran upstairs to get another photo album, the weight on my chest growing lighter with every step.

CHAPTER NINETEEN

Anna

A tear glided down my cheek. This was not at all what I'd expected. It was more wonderful and more horrible than what I'd imagined, like so many things in life.

I wiped the tear away and reached for my phone.

There was a message from my mom. "And???" she had written, followed by a second text five minutes later where she added, "?????"

Thanks to some helpful jokes from my dad, my mom was convinced I'd soon be kidnapped and taken to Moscow, so I had to answer. "Nothing bad. I'll explain later."

Leo walked back into the kitchen with a stack of albums in his arms. The mist in his eyes was gone, and he was smiling.

"Start with this one."

He handed me an album with a picture of newborn Oliver on the cover, and we spent the next half hour going through it. Then we repeated this process with two more albums.

I learned two things. First, Leo and his mom had spent months in Poland with Oliver, and second, Oliver was one of the most adorable babies who had ever lived. He had pudgy thighs, arm rolls, angelically chubby cheeks, and Leo's stunning blue eyes.

There was a fourth album, but I decided to ask some questions before we went through it.

"So, Leo..." I faced him. "What's my role in all of this?"

He opened his mouth to speak, but I interrupted him. "If it's to kidnap baby Oliver, I'm all for it. I think I can take the old woman."

He laughed. "Kidnapping won't be necessary. I've been in the process of adopting him for months. I started as soon as I'd heard about my brother's..."

Leo's voice trailed off, and I picked up the conversation. "Do adoptions usually take this long?"

"They normally take longer, but one of my friends from high school works in immigration and has been a huge help."

My phone lit up: a call from my mom. Apparently a text wasn't enough. She wanted a full explanation, *now*.

That's my family. Everything is *now, now, now,* you're going to be late, you're late, we're late!

She would have to wait.

I silenced the call and shook my head. "Nepotism."

"That's not nepotism! Nepotism was me helping my future brother-in-law get re-enrolled at Madison."

"What? That was you?" I stared at him. "I thought—"

He grinned. "Frankie never told you? I guess you're not the only member of your family who's good at keeping secrets."

"Yeah." Heat rushed to my cheeks. "Anyway, if Oliver is almost adopted, what do you need me for?"

"It's Agnieszka's aunt, Mrs. Sowka."

"*Pani* Sowka," I corrected.

He nodded. "Right. I've been calling her that."

"Is she Oliver's legal guardian?"

"Yes. Other than us, she's his only living relative." He pulled his phone out of his pocket. "I have a bunch of pictures here. Hang on a sec."

I watched as he opened a folder on his phone titled "Dr. Sowka."

A black and white picture of a smiling woman in a white coat filled the screen. "That's her when she was doing her residency in Canada."

I took the phone from him and zoomed in. "Residency! For what?"

"She's a pediatrician. Loves kids, but never had any of her own."

I felt a tightness in my chest. "Do you have more pictures?"

"Yeah. Go ahead, swipe through. She let me go through all her pictures, told me a bunch of stories. When she was in Canada another doctor proposed to her, and she almost said yes, but at the last minute she changed her mind. Never married."

A woman who loved kids but focused on her career. I could relate. "Is she really willing to let Oliver be adopted away from her like that?"

He pulled back and sighed. I hadn't realized how close he was to me, and a chill ran down my back.

"That's the problem," he said. "I wanted to adopt Oliver immediately, and in the beginning, she seemed okay with it. She's seventy years old – she's the first to admit she can't take care of him forever. But as the months went on, she started to get cold feet."

"Why?"

"A lot of reasons. She thinks Oliver should grow up in Poland. There's a family in town who wants to take him and..." He shook his head. "Most of all, she's said it's because I can't take care of him on my own, as a bachelor, a 'party boy,' as she called me."

A picture came up of her, this one in color, sitting at a desk with a placard that read *Head of Pediatrics.* "Ah."

"She thinks I'm a vagrant artist."

I laughed. "Aren't you?"

His jaw dropped and he put a hand to his chest. "Not anymore. I'm a respected professor."

"Oh, that's right." I nodded solemnly.

"I took the first job I could get, and here I am." His smile faded, staring at a picture of Oliver with Pani Sowka. "A few months ago, she said she was going to revoke the adoption, and I panicked. I told her I was getting married."

"I see." Oliver's little face smiled back at us. "Did you say it was to a Polish woman to sweeten the deal?"

He winced, raising a hand to scratch his eyebrow. "Yeah."

I crossed my arms over my chest. "All this time I thought you picked me because of my stunning beauty."

"That helped," he said.

"Ha. Right." I sat back, straightening my shoulders. I wasn't as tall or as thin or as good with makeup as whatever models he probably dated in New York City, but *dang it*, I could impress an old Polish woman. "When do I get to meet Pani Sowka?"

"Whenever you want. I've been visiting any chance I get – that's where I went last month during our Zermatt trip."

Oh. Was that what Ken had warned me about?

I let out a snort.

He cocked his head to the side, reminding me for a moment of an adorable Golden Retriever. "What?"

"I think Ken spied on you. He told me you were hiding something."

Leo stood and put his phone into his pocket. "Ken needs to learn to mind his business."

"I'm sorry!" I put my hands up. "I thought you'd think it was funny."

"No, I'm sorry," he said, his voice softening. "He can mess with me all he wants, but he's not going to mess with Oliver."

"He won't." I chanced a smile. "I'll get Lisa to keep him busy. They seemed to hit it off yesterday."

Leo's stony expression cracked into a smile. "She deserves better." He paused, reaching back into his pocket. "Hang on, I'm getting a call." He narrowed his eyes, then looked up at me. "It's your mom."

Now, now, now.

"How did she get my number?"

"I gave it to her. She has to have the number of anyone I spend time with so she can reach me at all hours." I sighed and reached out a hand. "Do you mind?"

"No, please." He handed the phone to me, and I hit accept.

"Hello, Mama," I said, dramatically drawing out *Mama*.

"Why aren't you answering your phone?"

Straight to business. "I'm with Leo. Everything is fine."

"Everything is not fine! Frankie is going to court!"

"What? Okay, why—"

She cut me off. "Those *snakes* are going to say he did it!"

"What snakes? What are you talking about?"

"Aren't you listening?" She sighed. "Brandon and Jamie. They are the snakes!"

We weren't getting anywhere with this conversation. "Is Frankie there?"

She was quiet, then said, "He doesn't want to talk to you."

I groaned. "Please get him on the phone."

I heard whispers and scuffling, and after a moment, Frankie spoke. "My lawyer thinks they made a deal. Brandon and Jamie made a deal with their lawyer to testify against me. They're going to say I did it all, that they weren't even involved."

"That's crazy!"

"My lawyer said they probably got a plea deal with probation, and I'll be the only one going to court."

My heart pounded in my chest, a sickly feeling washing over me. "I'm going to call him. Your lawyer."

He scoffed. "Oh yeah. Thanks a lot for convincing me to use a different lawyer from them. Worked out great. I'm going to spend the rest of my life in prison."

"Frankie, listen, I'm–"

The line went dead and my stomach dropped to my knees. I thrust the phone back into Leo's hands.

"Anna?" He stared at me with big eyes.

I fumbled with my purse, trying to pull out my phone. Did I need to call my mom? The lawyer? Ken?

"What happened?" Leo asked.

Tears rushed to my eyes and I pushed them away, swallowing against the lump in my throat. "I think, uh..." I took a breath. "I think I ruined my brother's life."

CHAPTER TWENTY

Leo

Brothers. A dismissal from a brother could devastate you like no one else. Dima had taught me that lesson again and again.

"You couldn't have ruined his life," I said. "What happened?"

Anna clutched her phone in her hands. "I don't know. I have to go." She got up to leave, then paused. "I'm sorry. Are we going to visit Oliver this weekend?"

"I'm flying out on Thursday night. I can buy you a ticket, but if you have things going on..."

"No." She offered a shaky smile. "I want to go. I'll text you?"

"Sure."

She grabbed her coat and disappeared through the front door, her minivan grumbling to a start a moment later.

Frankie was probably overreacting. He was young and life was more intense for young people. The emotions were bigger, the outcomes unimaginable.

Thinking on it, Dima was Frankie's age when my mom managed to get him a visa to come to the US. He refused it, as he always did, without a care as to how much work or money she'd put into it. She cried every night for a month.

I watched through the window as Anna pulled away, then, my limbs growing heavier with every step, returned to the kitchen.

I poured a fresh mug of coffee and took a seat. This morning, when I was lying in bed long before the sun rose, I was unable to imagine a positive outcome to telling Anna the truth. It was the youngest I'd felt in years – that is to say, the most dramatic. Was this what it was like to want something?

How unpleasant.

Beyond that, I knew what my history sounded like: a sob story. I hated sob stories. They were for people eliciting sympathy, and for people who couldn't take care of things on their own. I'd gone as far as I could with the adoption, though, and I'd hit an immovable wall: a stubborn Polish woman.

Anna was the answer. Another stubborn Polish woman. She had to be the answer.

She'd *gushed* over Oliver, poured over his pictures and raved about his smile, his eyes, and his absurdly round cheeks.

She could be faking it, but...why? How? I'd never particularly liked children, but Oliver had converted me. He was all charm, pure joy and laughter, and he was beautiful – beyond beautiful. He was everything. How could anyone stop short of loving him?

I stood and got my laptop. I'd buy Anna a plane ticket and she would see for herself.

• • •

We met at the airport late Thursday evening. I hadn't heard much from her, so I was unsure she'd show, but there she was, pulling a suitcase behind her. The skin under her eyes was a deep eggplant, and she hardly smiled when she saw me.

"Everything all right?" I asked.

"Yeah. You?"

I nodded. Whatever was going on, she wasn't ready to talk about it.

I didn't push, and as we went through security, she offered more. "Frankie's attorney assures me he's working on a plea deal of his own."

"That's good."

"Yeah, except everyone in the family blames me because Frankie doesn't *already* have a deal."

"Maybe they expect too much."

She removed her laptop from her bag and turned to me. "Maybe. Either way, it's the perfect time to leave the country."

"Running away from our problems never felt so right."

Anna laughed, then was promptly whisked away by a TSA agent.

I took my time getting my shoes off. Rushing was for the birds. We had a long trip ahead of us, but in the end, I'd get to see Oliver. That was all that mattered.

We got through security without issue and I bought us each a coffee.

"Is your mom going to be there?" Anna asked.

"She was there the last three weeks, but she just left. We try to alternate."

She looked down into the cardboard cup, creamer swirling into the coffee. "Ah."

Was she disappointed? No matter how many times I assured my mom Anna wasn't one to get scared off, she was still too terrified to meet her.

"It's better if I stay away," my mom would say. "Both me and your father."

I could agree with half of her statement. Anna and my mom would get along fine. My dad, on the other hand, could start a fight with anyone.

Thinking of it, I didn't know who would win in an argument between them. My dad would *think* he'd won, though, which would be insufferable enough.

We boarded the plane, hit our connection, and then took off for the longer leg of the trip. I thought I'd be too nervous to sleep, but as soon as they dimmed the cabin lights I passed out, waking when breakfast was served.

Anna was already awake, staring at her phone.

"What's up?"

She tucked it away. "Nothing. I paid for WiFi to see if anyone tried texting me, but...no one did."

"Oh." I sat up, unable to contain a yawn. "Family's still mad, huh?"

"Seems like it."

I poked her with my elbow. "Or were you waiting to hear from Ken?"

She rolled her eyes. "Yeah, right."

After breakfast, we watched a murder mystery on Anna's laptop. I tried to focus, but it lost my attention halfway through. My mind was elsewhere. We had a two-hour drive to Mielec, where Pani Sowka lived, and if we hurried, we could still see Oliver before he went to sleep that night.

As soon as we landed, we hurried off the plane and into the rental car. Anna didn't complain about me rushing her, which I appreciated, and even became chattier as we drove. She pointed out landmarks and told me about her relatives or the history of various towns.

I was happy to listen, and we didn't run into trouble until she started making demands.

"Pull over here," she said, pointing. "I need to buy flowers for Pani Sowka."

"There's no time." I kept driving.

She let out a gasp. "Leo!"

"It's fine. You don't need flowers."

She glared at me in silence for a moment. "If I don't show up with *nice* flowers, I might as well not show up at all."

"Oliver doesn't like flowers," I said, keeping the smile off my face.

"I will open this door and tumble into the road."

I looked over. Her hand was on the handle. "Don't do that."

She raised her eyebrows. "Next time I tell you to exit, *exit.*"

"If we're late, he'll be asleep when we get there and—"

She cut me off. "We won't be late! Just do it."

"Fine."

"Fine."

Twenty minutes later I pulled off the road, and within four minutes Anna came *sprinting* back to the car with an enormous bouquet in her arms.

She thudded into the passenger seat, tugging at tissue paper surrounding the flowers before shutting the door. "Go!"

"Did you steal those?" I asked.

"Wouldn't you like to know?" The flowers barely fit into the car and completely blocked her from my view. I heard the seatbelt click and she added, "Okay, drive!"

To her credit, she'd only added six minutes to our time and we got to Pani Sowka's house at seven. I slowed in front of her house and shut off the car.

"Are you ready for this?" I asked.

She brought the flowers forward. "I can't believe you've been letting me drive this whole time. You clearly know how to drive."

Driving in Poland was different. I didn't feel the pressure, and if anyone got angry, I could just throw my hands up and say, "Sorry, I'm from America."

I got out of the car. "I'll get the bags." I had a present for Oliver, but it would have to wait until the morning. Pani Sowka wouldn't appreciate us riling up Oliver before bed.

Would this be the time he forgot me? The first time my face made him cry instead of smile?

I'd been reading about separation anxiety and stranger danger in nine month olds, and as much as I told myself it shouldn't crush me if Oliver's lip started to quiver when he saw me, I knew it would.

"You okay?" Anna asked, peering over. She'd walked to the back of the car silently.

"Yeah. Why? Are you okay?"

"Yeah. Excited." She put a hand on my shoulder. "We're a good team. We've got this."

Right. She needed to be convincing. I hadn't wasted any time worrying about that. Anna was a professional.

And she'd bought those flowers.

I grabbed both of our bags and shut the trunk, only taking one step when I felt Anna's hand reach into mine.

I looked at her and she smiled.

A team. I smiled back. "Here we go."

CHAPTER TWENTY-ONE

Anna

Leo unlocked the front door and we stepped inside. It was a small house, the entryway cramped with coats and shoes, the windows covered with heavy curtains. There was an amber light down the hallway in what looked like the kitchen, and a second light atop a narrow staircase.

We took off our shoes as Leo called out a hello in Polish.

"Is that the only word you know?" I asked in a low voice.

He leaned down to tuck his shoes away and brushed my arm on his way up. "I also know how to say my mother is from Poland and how to ask for beer."

Goosebumps rippled across my arm. His face was in a shadow, just as it was when he'd leaned in to kiss me at the party. My mind kept going back to that moment, playing it over and over, forcing the air to escape from my lungs.

"*We're upstairs,*" a voice, presumably Pani Sowka, yelled back in Polish.

Leo flashed a smile at me before dropping the bags and running up the stairs.

I'd never seen him so excited. In fact, I don't think I'd seen him more than mildly amused, and that was usually when he was messing with me.

I dropped the flowers and ran after him, reaching the top of the darkened hallway. There was a bathroom to the right, the door open, and two other doors on the other side of the hall.

Leo stepped into the first doorway and I followed.

"Hello," Leo said, then, switching to English and a high voice, added, "Who's there? Is that Oliver?"

A squeal rang out, and Oliver came into view as Leo stepped forward. He was dressed in a onesie, light blue with puffy white clouds, his bare feet sticking out, toes pointed. He sat in the lap of an older woman, her hair twisted and pinned, a grin on her face.

"It can't be. He's too big." Leo stood with his hands on his hips, shaking his head.

Oliver laughed, flashing a nearly-toothless smile, and reached his arms toward Leo. In one swift motion, Leo picked Oliver up, swung him upside down and planted a kiss on his cheek. Oliver shrieked with glee, clinging to Leo like a baby koala.

I couldn't look away. Not only was Oliver a perfect cherub with fat cheeks and fat arms and rounded croissant feet (seriously, what is it with baby feet? Is it the length-to-height ratio? The fatness makes the cuteness?), but seeing Leo drop his cool artist act and turn into a baby whisperer was too much.

"Hello, I'm Anna," I said, smiling and waving at Pani Sowka like a fool.

Pani Sowka smiled back at me. She was a pretty lady, her hair dyed an ashy blonde, her makeup delicate and highlighting her round blue eyes. She stood and kissed me once on the cheek. *"Welcome!"*

When I stepped back, Oliver was staring at me. His smile had faded into a suspicious scowl.

"Hi, sweetheart," I said, keeping my voice low.

Oliver's brow furrowed. He looked at Leo, then to me, then back to Leo before taking one little hand and tapping Leo on the cheek.

"Yes, I need to shave," Leo said with a sigh. "I'm sorry. Long trip, buddy."

I had to pinch my lips together to contain a whimper. It was too much. I'll admit Leo is attractive with his swoopy dark hair, his shining blue eyes, and his sharp facial features.

He's hot. So what? There are tons of hot guys. Millions, probably.

But when a hot guy delicately cradles a little baby like that, carrying on a conversation? And the baby likes him and touches his face and smiles a gummy smile?

Just carry me away.

"He's a little afraid, but he'll warm up," Pani Sowka said.

"I don't want to scare him." I smiled at her. "Leo, are you going to put him to sleep?"

He nodded, grinning as Oliver's face taps progressed to more aggressive baby slaps. He grabbed Oliver's hand and gently pulled it toward me. "Go ahead, Oliver. Say goodnight to Anna."

I popped forward, planting a kiss on Oliver's hand, and he promptly pulled it away.

We all laughed, and Oliver started laughing too, clearly in on the joke.

I took a step toward the doorway and Pani Sowka followed, stopping to add in heavily accented English, "Oliver must be in bed in ten minutes."

Leo nodded. "Okay, got it. Thank you."

She walked out of the room and I followed.

"*Leo says you are a professor?*" she asked over her shoulder.

"*Almost,*" I said. "*I'm still working on it.*"

Working on it, was that how to say it? I cursed myself for not making a point to practice my Polish before coming out here. It got rusty so quickly.

She reached the kitchen and grabbed a towel before turning to me. "*Engineering?*"

I nodded, stooping to pick up my monstrous bouquet of flowers in the entryway. Their potent scent was more tolerable outside of the car. "*I like it very much.*" I smiled, thrusting the bouquet forward. "*The flowers are for you.*"

She accepted them, touching the blooms approvingly. "*How beautiful! Thank you.*"

She motioned for me to sit, then disappeared into a side room, emerging a moment later with a vase.

I looked around the kitchen. It was small but impeccably clean, with a fridge that would be considered a minifridge back home, a small sink, and a window lined with flowers and plants.

"*Leo told me you are still working? As a doctor?*"

"Just a few days a week. I'm an old woman." She laughed, putting the flowers into the vase, fluffing them slightly before motioning for me to follow. *"Come. We'll put these on the table."*

She didn't move like an old woman. She moved like she'd been shot out of a barrel.

I followed her into the next room, another tight space. It was filled by a large table and eight chairs. I could imagine many late nights of food, booze, and arguing at this table. Tonight, it was covered with a white tablecloth, three places set with wine glasses at the ready.

She set the flowers down and stood back, admiring them. *"Lovely!"* she said in English, grinning.

We walked back to the kitchen, and I stood dumbly by as she stirred soup, cut dill, and asked me questions. I told her about my schooling, where we lived, and my siblings.

Eventually, the questioning circled back to my family history.

"Where are your parents from?" she asked.

"My dad is from Kliszów, and my mom was born in Radomyśl Wielki."

She turned me, eyes bright. *"What's your mother's name?"*

"Agata Makowski, but she was Agata Ptak."

Pani Sowka clapped her hands together. *"Your grandparents are Stanley and Mary Ptak?"*

I smiled. *"You knew them?"*

She threw her head back and clapped her hands together. *"Knew them? They lived down the street from me. I grew up admiring your grandma!"*

That was all it took. When Leo came downstairs, he could barely get a word in. Pani Sowka and I were going back and forth, her talking a mile a minute, and me chiming in with my broken Polish. I was no longer self-conscious about how I sounded. She understood me well enough and didn't make a point of correcting me.

"Oliver's almost asleep," Leo announced, waving the monitor in his hand.

We stopped talking and looked at him. Pani Sowka said, *"Good,"* then went back to a story about my grandma smuggling fabric into the country during communism.

My grandma had been what the kids would call a hustler. She had to be, because even though her husband was an educated man (a dentist!), they didn't have much under communism, and the government took much of his earnings.

As my mom likes to say, "Under communism, everyone has the same: nothing."

My grandma and grandpa (aka Babcia and Dziadziu) traveled all around, buying and selling whatever they could. They bought gold rings in Egypt, crystal in Czechoslovakia, and electronics from Russia, smuggling them back into Poland, often waiting in line for days at the border to sneak the goods through. Every vacation was a low-key business trip, every border crossing an adventure.

They did it all. Illegally, of course, but what good are rules when the rules are stupid?

The fabric story was one I hadn't heard before. Apparently, Babcia had gotten a good deal on some fine silk, and to get it across the border, she'd made Dziadziu wrap it around his torso under his clothes.

This fooled no one.

Pani Sowka was in tears retelling the story. *"When the guards unwound him, he was livid. He said to your grandmother, 'I am not taking you on vacation ever again!'"*

We erupted into laughter and Leo stared at us.

"Sorry," I said, patting him on the shoulder. "I'll tell you later."

Pani Sowka stood up, patting him on the other shoulder. "We are almost ready for dinner." Then she looked at me. *"What are you drinking?"*

I shrugged. *"Water, but I can get it."*

"No, sit!" She paused, adding, *"And a little wine,"* with a wink before disappearing into the kitchen.

Leo crossed his arms and let out a dramatic sigh. "Did you just order a drink without me?"

"There's no ordering," I said in a low voice. "We are all getting wine."

He laughed. "Sounds about right."

"How's Oliver? It looked like he was happy to see you."

"Yeah." Leo grinned. "I'm just glad he remembers me."

"He'll always remember you. He loves you!"

Leo scratched the back of his head, still beaming. "I hope so."

Pani Sowka returned carrying a tray with an enormous plate of open-faced sandwiches, three shot glasses spilling over with brown liquid, and a bottle of wine. She set it down and handed out the shot glasses. "A cheers for Oliver," she said proudly, holding up a shot glass.

Though my travel stomach didn't appreciate liquor, I wasn't going to offend her. I held up the glass. "For Oliver!"

Leo repeated the toast, and I leaned back, the familiar burn of warm brandy hitting my throat.

I smiled to myself. Dziadziu had loved pulling out a bottle of room-temperature brandy for his guests. Was Pani Sowka paying homage to him? Or was this an old tradition from Radomyśl?

Before I could ask, Pani Sowka gathered the spare glasses and disappeared.

"She's fast," I said to Leo.

"And really likes you, apparently. What were you two talking about?"

"Oh." I smiled. "She knows my grandparents. They grew up in the same city."

He shook his head. "I knew it. You all know each other."

"We do not!" I lowered my voice. "It's destiny."

"Nah." He waved a hand. "Just a good return on my investment."

I snorted a laugh as Pani Sowka returned with a vat of her homemade chicken soup. After that, we had a feast of pork cutlets, mashed potatoes, green beans (frozen from her garden and thawed just for the occasion), and a lemon cake for dessert.

We spent three hours talking and laughing at the table, me and Pani Sowka trying to stick to English, and Leo finally getting to be in on the jokes.

I didn't think he minded too much. He smiled a lot, he laughed a lot, and every chance he had, he snuck a glance at the baby monitor.

It's enough to make a woman melt, if that were something I did.

. . .

The next morning, I asked Pani Sowka not to tell my relatives I was in Poland, as they would be deeply offended I was visiting with Oliver and not with them.

"*Child,*" she said, grabbing my arm, "*I won't say a word.*"

Oliver was in a chipper mood, only giving me the stink eye for thirty minutes before deciding he wanted to babble and make faces at me.

We spent the next two days as a happy little family, walking to town in the brisk, clean air, eating at restaurants, and shopping at the little stores. It was like something out of a dream, enough to make me forget that my family was furious with me and hadn't spoken to me the entire time (except for my mom, who asked if I'd made it, and then broke down her icy walls after a video call from Oliver).

It was so nice, in fact, that I decided to extend my visit. I emailed Carl to see what he thought, and he enthusiastically encouraged me to take a month off.

"You've never taken a single vacation day in years," he said, "and we're just waiting on the comments for the paper. Have fun! Send pictures!"

The poor man still thought I was a runaway girl in love, and though the guilt was heavy, I accepted his offer.

Not the full month– that was too much – and in two weeks, I had a meeting with Frankie's lawyer I fully intended to keep.

On Sunday, I talked to Pani Sowka, and she enthusiastically offered to let me stay with her and Oliver. The only person who didn't seem happy about my change of plans was Leo, and I had no idea why.

"I don't understand why you are changing our plans, or why you need to stay so long," he said as he packed his bag to leave.

"It's not that long," I argued. "It's two weeks. Pani Sowka has to work a few shifts and said she could use the help with Oliver, and ... I don't know, we're having a nice time."

He shoved clothes into his bag and zipped it shut. "This isn't a vacation, you know. You were supposed to convince her we're a real couple, then make an exit."

"Right, because running out of here after three days is *really* convincing."

He shot me a look as he walked toward the doorway. "Just don't mess it up."

I could feel the heat rising in my chest, but I had to keep my voice down. Pani Sowka was just downstairs. "I'm not going to mess anything up. I'm getting to know Oliver, so if you need help when you get him to Wisconsin, I can be there. I can babysit."

"I already have a nanny lined up." He stopped and turned to face me. His eyes were hard, his expression flat. "The adoption should be finalized soon. You won't have to worry about us."

"Oh." I took a step back, a weight pressing into my chest. "Okay."

He nodded once, then spun and walked into the hallway.

Were we still playing happy couple? I had nothing else to cling to, so I followed him downstairs, standing silent and dumb behind him.

"Goodbye, Pani Sowka," he said, kissing her on the cheek. "I'll be back soon."

She sighed, wiping her hands on her apron. "Very good, Leo."

He was about to leave when he stopped himself, leaning in to kiss me on the cheek. "Don't forget to call."

It wasn't the kiss I'd been hoping for. "I won't."

He left through the front door and I locked it behind him. When I turned around, Pani Sowka was watching me. Her eyes were a little too narrow and a little too knowing.

"He's nervous about the trip," I said.

She stared at me for a beat before responding. *"He's always upset when he has to leave."*

I wanted to believe her. I wanted to push the heavy feeling out of my chest. *"Yes."*

"Don't worry." She clasped her hands together. *"Are you hungry?"*

I nodded and she turned, waving me into the kitchen.

Whatever his problem was, I still needed to play my role. There was a plate of sliced meat with my name on it, and if I hurried, I could beat Pani Sowka to making the tea.

I took a deep breath and forced a smile.

CHAPTER TWENTY-TWO

Leo

Why couldn't Anna just stick to the plan? Fly in, play with Oliver, charm Pani Sowka, leave. There'd been more than enough charming going on. It was time to go.

It irritated me, and I didn't know why. Her being able to spend so much time with Oliver sparked some jealousy, but there was more than that. I couldn't put my finger on it, and it nagged at me for the entire trip home.

I tried distracting myself on the flight by listening to music and watching movies, but nothing worked. My mind kept circling back to how her plan came into being without even asking me.

That, too, was rude, but it wasn't everything.

By the time I got home, I gave up on trying to figure out *why* exactly it bothered me so much. The reason didn't matter, since Anna wouldn't listen to me anyway, and I had other things to focus on. I needed to get the house ready for Oliver.

My lawyer said we were close to finalizing the adoption, and depending on when things were approved, we could find out in a matter of weeks – even days – that Oliver was coming home.

The one benefit of Anna staying behind was she was much better at video calling than Pani Sowka, and it was hard to stay angry at her when she called me twice a day, every day.

Seeing Oliver's smiling little face was like a balm. The calls got me through two weeks of worrying about his passport, the foreign custody decree, and forms I-600 and I-600a, all while dealing with students who'd decided to band together to demand extra credit.

There was nothing more irritating than entitled students. Four of them marched into my office one morning with a list of demands, telling me what they "deserved."

If they'd asked nicely, I would've given them all A's. What did I care? I, too, had once ridden on the hubris of youth, sure the world would come to heel.

Now I was an old man, about to become a father. I decided to practice my dad jokes on them, telling them to write a four-hundred-word essay on the most artistically perfect Nicolas Cage movie and get back to me.

"Which movie is it?" they demanded to know.

"Ah," I said as I rushed them out the door, "that is for you to figure out."

I was a different sort of professor than my dad. In his mind, I taught the equivalent of cave drawings while he solved the universe's problems with math.

He missed the point, like he always did. Theater, paintings, poetry, movies – none of that moved him because they weren't equations. Formulas. He'd spent the last eight months telling me the adoption was a bad idea, how it didn't add up, that they would realize I was an unfit father, that it would fall apart at the last second.

He was wrong about so many things, but the adoption most of all. It was real, it was happening, and it was right.

I hadn't painted in months, but now I couldn't stop. I stayed awake into the late hours, working under lights I'd rigged, fueled by the thrill and terror of a dream come to life.

The paintings weren't anything I could sell. Nothing that would make my agent happy. It was all for Oliver.

It wouldn't mean much to him now, but maybe one day he'd see the paintings and roll his eyes as I retold the story of how he came to be my son.

CHAPTER TWENTY-THREE

Anna

My return flight from Kraków was complicated by a fourteen-hour delay, leaving me only an hour to get from the airport to the lawyer's office.

I texted Frankie and asked if he wanted to come along, but he never answered. The only person in my family who was still speaking to me was my mom, and that was all thanks to Oliver. She was a sucker for babies – I now understood how she ended up with four – and out of all the babies, Oliver was king.

He was the sweetest, cuddliest, smiliest baby in Poland, and possibly all of Europe. He adored reading (Leo had supplied an impressive supply of books in English, Sandra Boynton being the favorite), he loved going for walks to town and babbling at the shopkeepers, and he lived for crawling in the grass and squealing at bugs.

I missed him the moment I left Pani Sowka's house, but I had to get back to real life, even if no one was particularly pleased with me at the moment – maybe especially so.

I got to the lawyer's office seven excruciating minutes late, out of breath and oozing sweat after my jog from the parking lot. "Hi, I'm Anna. I am *so* sorry I'm late. I hope he can still see me."

The secretary gave me a stiff smile. "I'll let him know you're here. Have a seat."

She turned back to her computer, typing something, then said something about a swimsuit she'd bought for a cruise.

I looked at her, wide-eyed, unsure how to contribute to the conversation, and realized she was talking to someone on a video call on her phone.

Awkward, but at least it wasn't me being awkward for once.

After thirty minutes, I was forced to interrupt her riveting conversation comparing halter tops to bikinis.

"Excuse me, is he here? Or should I come back?"

"He'll get to you when he can," she said sweetly.

Another twenty minutes went by, and I got the brilliant idea of calling the man myself.

He picked up after six rings. "Edgar B., attorney at law, at your service."

He'd never answered like that before. "Edgar?"

"You've got him."

"This is Anna Makowski. I had an appointment to meet with you about my brother's case."

"I'm actually at the office now. Come on by."

I looked around. "You are? I'm in the waiting room and I haven't seen you."

The wooden door directly across from where I was sitting flew open, Edgar stumbling out. His white shirt was unbuttoned, exposing the graying hair on his chest, and his belt was hanging open.

He widened his arms when he saw me. "Anna!"

He took a step closer, and that's when the smell hit me. Hot, sweaty onions – what I've learned is old vodka seeping out of pores.

I stood from my seat and stepped back, shooting a glance at the secretary. She'd looked up at this interaction, but promptly returned to talking on the phone as if nothing unusual had occurred.

By the time I looked back, he had his arms around me in a gripping hug. I was too stunned to pull away, my arms pinned at my sides, my breath held tight.

He leaned back to look at me and a drop of sweat jumped from his forehead, cascaded through the air, and landed on the bridge of my nose.

I snapped myself away, breaking his grasp. "Ew!"

"Aw, Anna, dear Anna – "

"No!" I said, louder, wagging a finger at him like he was a Saint Bernard who had gotten frisky. "*What* are you doing?"

"Oh come on, you gotta have a little fun sometimes." He said the last word with a long drawl, as if it had gotten stuck in his mouth.

I brushed my jacket with my hands. I could feel his sweat seeping in like a marinade. It would never be clean again. I'd have to throw it away, burn it maybe. "You're supposed to be working on my brother's case."

"I *am* hard at work." He nodded, pressing his lips into a frown. "Murder cases do this to me. I get so busy saving lives, I need to bring a little joy back into the world."

I took a deep breath. "My brother is not a murder suspect. Frank Makowski. Do you know who I'm talking about?"

"Honey, I've got so many clients, you wouldn't believe. Let me take you out to dinner sometime, I'll tell you all about it."

He leaned in, shining his yellowing teeth in a wide grin, his eyes red and veiny. His hand reached for my shoulder and missed, so I took the opportunity to step away.

"I would rather swim in a pool filled with vodka," I said, stepping backward. "Which seems like what you've been doing all morning."

I turned to leave, stopping with my hand on the door. "Also, you're fired."

I slammed the door on my way out, rushing to my car in a huff.

How could he be *so* egregiously awful and get such rave reviews? His secretary didn't even bat an eyelash at the scene in front of her. It had to be his usual behavior...but everyone said he was the best criminal defense attorney in the city!

I got to my car and threw the soiled jacket into the passenger seat. I needed to find a new attorney, and it needed to happen immediately. The trial date was supposed to be set this week, and once that ball started rolling, there was no stopping it.

I texted Lisa. Though she would deny it to the family, she'd been talking to me as if nothing had happened, convinced everyone would get over their anger eventually.

"Frankie's lawyer is a bust. Can you reach out to your lawyer network to get new referrals?"

"How are we going to pay for it?" she wrote back.

Shoot. Good point.

I called Leo. "Hey, are you busy?"

"Just in my office. What's up? Did you finally make it back?"

"Yeah." I started the car. "We need to talk."

He lowered his voice. "What's wrong? Is it Pani Sowka?"

"No, we're best friends. It's Frankie's lawyer – he ruined my favorite jacket with his vodka sweat juice."

"What?"

It was too hard for my brain to talk, drive, and panic at the same time, so I had to end the call. "I'll be there in half an hour."

"Okay. See you soon."

The drive did the opposite of settling my mind, and I burst into Leo's office like a tornado, throwing the door open and startling the student sitting inside.

"Oh," I said when I saw her jump. "Sorry."

"Hey." Leo waved. "We were discussing the artistic merits of Nic Cage. Do you want to give us your take on *National Treasure?*"

I stared at him, and he spoke again.

"Or are you telling me you don't care about the Declaration of Independence being stolen?"

"Uh." I looked at Leo, then the student. "No."

Leo leaned against his desk, as casual as can be. "Personally, the terror and confusion that peaks at the end of *The Wicker Man* has always haunted me, but we've been having a candid argument about Nic's moving performance in *Face/Off*."

Was it a full moon or something? What was he talking about? "Do you want me to come back later?"

"No, I think we're done." He laughed. "Thanks for your thoughtful effort. You've got an A."

The student jumped up from her seat. "Thank you!"

"Enjoy the day."

She left with a spring in her step, and I tossed my purse to the floor and took her seat. "Hey."

He tilted his head to the side. "You okay?"

"No. I just got back from seeing Frankie's attorney. I was waiting for an hour while the secretary kept just chewing gum and talking about swimsuits."

"Sounds unpleasant."

"The lawyer finally came out and he was *stinking* drunk, and he hit on me and had no idea who I was."

Leo held up a finger. "Just because he was drunk doesn't mean he's not a good attorney." He paused. "And he clearly has great taste."

"That's not funny," I snapped. "I fired him, and I need to find someone else right away."

Leo nodded, taking a seat behind his desk. "Right now?"

"Yeah. I need to hire someone, figure out how to transfer the case, and – don't get mad – I need the rest of the money so I can pay this new person."

He sat back, staring at me.

"What?"

More staring, until he finally spoke. "Have you ever thought maybe you should involve Frankie in these decisions?"

I rolled my eyes. "Yeah, like he's in the right place to handle that right now."

Leo brushed a strand of hair away from his brilliant, focused eyes.

"What?" I asked. "Spit it out."

He clasped his hands on the desk. "I don't feel good about this."

"What's not to feel good about?"

He stood and walked to the bookshelf, turning his back to me, and I followed him, starting again. "You told me yourself the adoption is almost finalized. You don't have to worry that I'm going to, like, run off with the money."

He spun around. "Are you sure about that?"

"I just spent the last two weeks with Pani Sowka. You're welcome, by the way, for convincing her we'd make great parents."

"I didn't ask you to do that."

"Oh really? You didn't ask me to lie to a sweet woman, take on all that guilt, and keep up the lie with my family until they were convinced I was having a mental breakdown?"

"I didn't know you were going to stay there for two weeks. You came up with that on your own."

"So?"

"You can't just do whatever you want to do without considering other people, Anna! And yeah, how am I supposed to know you're not going to just take the rest of the money and disappear?"

Unbelievable. "Are you serious? Do you hear yourself? I've spent the last two weeks taking care of Oliver. Do you really think I would do that to him?"

"Even if you don't, did you ever think he doesn't need someone coming into his life, only to abandon him?"

I stopped. It had felt like I was building a successful little sandcastle of an argument, but now a wave had crashed in, taking out the seaside wall. "I'm not going to abandon him."

He shook his head. "Come on, Anna. You've gotten him attached to you, and for what?"

It was never a sandcastle, it was a mud castle. I wasn't on a sunny beach in a bikini and a big hat, I was in the middle of the Atlantic, standing on a rock, alone.

"Leo..."

I took a breath. Things had been going too well. After he kissed me, in front of everyone, and we went to Poland and pretended to be this happy little family...

Couldn't we go on pretending to be engaged forever? Maybe just until Oliver went to college? We could buy a pretend house, go on pretend vacations, get pretend pictures with the pretend Easter bunny and the real Santa?

Oliver loved bunnies; his favorite book was pictures of bunnies with facts. Didn't Leo think it would be nice? Didn't he think maybe we could make it work?

I wanted to say all of that, in a less crazy-sounding way, but all I could do was swallow hard against the bubble of embarrassment forming in my throat.

"I'm not going to abandon him," I repeated.

"Yes, you are. That's how this whole thing is supposed to work, don't you remember? That's what you agreed to. That's the entire reason I hired you."

Hired me. I was a seasonal worker, an actress, someone who was supposed to disappear at the end of the day.

My face started to burn, and I knew tears were coming. I couldn't do it in front of him, the man who had specifically paid me to *not* get attached, to not fall in love with his smile or his mesmerizing eyes or his adorable baby.

I shook my head. "I'm sorry."

Forcing a smile as I walked out the door, I left, running once I got into the parking lot, running away from my stupid, tender, gushy heart and the shame encased inside.

• • •

I managed to hold back the sobs until I got to my car, and then, afraid some well-meaning person might try to talk to me, I did the only thing an adult woman crying in her minivan could do: I went to my mom's house.

"Hello?" I called out as I walked through the door. "Is anyone home?"

A head popped up at the top of the stairs. Frankie.

Apparently, he'd had the same idea as me.

"Hey," I said.

He looked me up and down, his face unsmiling. "What's the matter with you?"

"It's been a rough day."

He nodded, walking halfway down the stairs before pausing. He'd let his hair grow out, and it looked so much like when he was eleven and had insisted on cutting it himself. It made me want to hug him, but I knew he wasn't in the mood to hug me, just like everyone else.

"I have some bad news about your lawyer."

He raised an eyebrow. "Yeah?"

"He's got a drinking problem." I paused, struggling to form my thoughts, then added, "But don't worry, I'm going to find someone else."

Frankie let out a breath and dropped down, hitting the step with a thud. "What happened, Anna?"

"I went to see him, and he was so drunk and–"

"He's not a drunk, Anna! He had a plan for how we were going to deal with my defense."

I looked away. "Well, he's gone. We're going to keep looking and..."

"*What* did you do?" He shook his head and stood. "He said we're going to trial next month. They're going to pick a jury soon. Why do you always do this?"

"I'm trying to help you, Frankie!"

"I don't need your help!" he bellowed, shooting to his feet and standing over me. "I'm not ten years old! You think you're helping, but you make everything worse!"

Tears sprung back to my eyes, spilling onto my dry, tight cheeks. "No, listen..."

"Do you know why Sarah moved to Chicago? It was to get away from you. She couldn't stand how you butted into her business and told her how to raise her kids."

"I don't tell her how to raise her kids!"

"You think you know everything, but you don't." He rubbed his face with his hand, then looked up. "Why can't you just leave us alone?"

He stormed up the stairs and slammed his bedroom door.

I stood there for a long time. The house was still and quiet, but everything looked at rest. At peace.

The only thing out of place was me. I should've been used to the feeling, but I wasn't. Not here.

All my life, I'd never quite fit. All the other kids just *knew* things. They knew the words to American songs. They knew all the Disney princesses and understood how football worked. They were allowed to wear makeup and have sleepovers.

I didn't think I was all that different, but I was. I never found a way to fit in. I was always a little off, a little awkward, a little strange.

The only place I fit was at home. It was where I was needed, where things had made sense – until now.

I didn't fit here anymore. I didn't fit anywhere. No one needed me. Worse, no one *wanted* me.

I turned and made the drive back to my apartment. Alone.

CHAPTER TWENTY-FOUR

Leo

There was no point in arguing. Anna knew I was right. Oliver had already lost his mother, his father, and soon he was going to lose Pani Sowka, the only constant figure he'd known.

What was I supposed to do, pretend to be happy after Anna had gained his trust, then took the money and moved on with her life?

He didn't need that. He didn't need any of it, and as much as my dad liked to tell me what a terrible father I was going to be, I would never abandon Oliver the way he had abandoned us again and again.

That was what bothered me so much. I couldn't let Oliver suffer any more abandonment, and it had never even crossed her mind. It was all a game to her.

We didn't need Anna. We didn't need anyone – except maybe Pani Sowka, if she'd agree to spend a few weeks in Madison to help Oliver transition.

On my way home from work, I stopped at the bank and wired Anna the rest of the money. If she decided to stick around and help with Oliver when he got here, that would be fine. If not, I never had to see her again.

. . .

A week and a half later, I got the call. The paperwork was approved, the I's were dotted, the T's were crossed, and all I had to do was fly to Poland and get my son.

I could've cried, but instead I pulled out the checklist my lawyer had me create for this moment. It listed next steps, what to do, whom to talk to, what to bring. Things to not forget.

Even still, it was hard to follow. My mind was spilling over with thoughts, and every time I tried to focus on the list, all I could think about was telling everyone the good news. My mom. My dad, just to hear him grumble about it. Pani Sowka.

Anna.

It was impossible not to think about her. After she'd realized I'd sent her the rest of the money, she sent me a text. "Thank you. I'm here whenever you need me. I won't do anything else without you telling me. I'm really sorry."

I didn't know what to say, so I had just replied, "Cool, thanks."

I hadn't heard from her since. Was she off with Ken now? Had she found a new lawyer for Frankie? Had the trial started?

She left only my imagination to fill in the blanks. In the course of a day, I could go from thinking she had been sorry to thinking she'd faked it all and had run off to be a billionaire bride.

After torturing myself for a few hours, I decided to call her. I wanted to see what she would say, or if she'd respond at all. Had she cared about Oliver, or had it all been an act?

She answered after two rings, her voice small and far away. "Hey."

"Hi. Anna?"

She cleared her throat. "How are you? How are things?"

"Things are great. I just got word that everything is in place for the adoption. I'm making plans to get out there and pick Oliver up. I think Pani Sowka might agree to come back if she can get some time off."

"That's amazing!" Her voice brightened. "I'm so happy to hear that."

I cleared my throat. "Yeah."

"Do you..." her voice broke, then started again. "Can I come, or would that not be helpful?"

I didn't see why not. It was always helpful to have another set of hands, and Oliver liked her well enough. "No, uh, I think that would be nice."

"Awesome!" She paused. "I was actually thinking...I have an idea, but I wanted to run it by you first."

Of course she had an idea. I tried to keep the edge out of my voice. "Okay?"

"We could take Ken's plane. I haven't asked him yet, but it would be a lot faster. We could fly directly to Mielec and back, and we wouldn't have to risk getting delayed like I did last time."

"Oh. Wow. That would solve a lot of problems, actually. It would be a lot easier for Oliver. A *lot* easier."

"And for Pani Sowka," she said. "She told me she doesn't even want to fly to London anymore because it takes too long."

I laughed. "Yeah, that sounds like her."

"Do you know when you want to go? Just send me the dates and I'll do the rest."

"Oh, okay." It was that easy? She and Ken must've become closer since he showed up at our engagement party.

I knew she'd end up with him. I just thought she'd wait until Oliver was here.

"I wanted to say I'm sorry about before," she added.

At least she was thinking of Oliver now. He wouldn't have to suffer through hours and hours of flying, transfers, and delays. I wasn't going to ask for more. "Don't worry about it."

"No, you were right," she said. "I gave Frankie the money so he could hire his own attorney. The trial is supposed to start next month."

"Did he find someone?"

"I think so. I don't know. I don't think I'm even allowed to come to the trial. It looks like..." Her voice cracked. "It doesn't look good for him."

My heart sank. "I'm sorry, Anna."

"It's not your fault. Anyway, I'll give Ken a call now. Text me when you're thinking, okay?"

"Sure. Will do."

She ended the call, leaving me with a feeling of unease in my chest.

CHAPTER TWENTY-FIVE

Anna

I t felt like someone was pushing their fist into my breast-bone – a dull, steady ache. I would've thought it was a heart attack if it hadn't started the moment Frankie looked at me with those disgusted eyes and said, "Just leave us alone."

I dragged the pain around for days before turning to the internet. Searching "pain in chest" didn't help, so I decided to broaden the search with "Why am I this way?"

Surprisingly, this led to answers. After a lot of clicking, and being distracted by videos of puppies and babies for two hours, I found real, gut-punching stuff.

Thanks to Frankie and Leo's helpful statements, I was able to narrow down not only what my problem was, but also what caused it. It had all started in my childhood. (Do enough inter-net searching and you'll find just about all your annoying and aberrant behaviors stem from childhood).

Apparently, in my formative years, I found validation in helping others. I helped my mom with her cleaning business, I helped my siblings with their lunches and homework and getting to the bus on time, and now that was the only way I felt worthy of love – to do everything for everyone, all the time, whether they liked it or not.

Sad, isn't it? But I think anyone would look sad through the lens of their late-night internet searches.

It wasn't *that* bad. Supposedly, it could be fixed. For other people, though. Not for me.

I was a lost cause.

I'd ruined Frankie's life. He was going to spend the next sixty years in jail. My mom would worry herself into an early grave and force my dad to concoct a Scooby Doo-type scheme to bust Frankie out of jail. He'd get caught, and then my next crazy relative would concoct *their* scheme to bust them out of jail.

I didn't know exactly how it would go down. I just knew it was all my fault.

There was no way to make up for the damage I'd caused, and that wasn't what I was trying to do by helping with Oliver's trip. I loved Oliver. I was doing it for him, not for me.

I made the call to Ken immediately, which might've been unwise since I didn't think about how to word my request – but honestly, I'm not great at wording things, so it would've been awkward either way.

I expected an assistant to answer, but Ken's voice boomed through the droning sound in the background. "Anna! It's so nice to hear from you."

"Hey Ken. Long time no talk."

See? I'm practically a poet.

"Hang on. We're testing our new helicopter prototype. I'll tell the pilot to take a break." He yelled out, and the buzzing stopped. "To what do I owe this pleasure?"

Who talks like that? Immigrant children don't learn flowery language like that. At least I hadn't. I could, however, confidently make dentist appointments for everyone in the family by age eight. "Well, Ken, I'm sort of like that terrible friend who only calls when they need something. And when I say sort of, I mean exactly like that."

He laughed. "The great Anna Makowski needs something from *me?* I'm flattered."

Before I could stop myself, I said, "I need a lot of things, Ken." I let out a nervous laugh. "Not your problem, of course, but – ah – here's the thing. Leo's going through the process to adopt his orphaned nephew."

"I know."

Oh. I guess he had been spying. Weird.

I cleared my throat. "We got word it's time to pick him up, and I was hoping to avoid a horrible multi-day journey for the kid."

"Say no more. My planes are just sitting around. Please take one."

That was easy. One of these days, this guy was going to wake up and realize how much he hated me, just like everyone else who knew me.

Luckily, today was not that day.

"That's a relief. Thank you, Ken. Is there any way I can repay you? Can I leave a review somewhere?"

He let out a hmm, then, "I've always wanted someone to send me one of those fruit bouquets."

"Done." I knew he was joking, but I didn't care. I'd send him one for every day of the week. He'd be drowning in chocolate covered strawberries by Christmas.

"There's another thing you could do," he added.

"Yeah?"

"Leave your fiancé. He doesn't deserve you."

You'd think I'd be more used to people being forward, since I liked being forward. You would be wrong.

My jaw hung open. "Uh..."

Why did this guy like me so much? What was his problem? Did he know what his problem was? Had he searched the internet, bleary eyed, reading about why he hurt everyone around him again and again? Or was that a me thing?

"I'm going to be honest," I said. "I don't know what you see in me, Ken. Frankly, I'm worried about you."

A laugh burst from him. "I appreciate your concern."

"You're welcome."

"But tell me, Anna. How is your and Leo's relationship?"

"It's fine." I chewed on my bottom lip. What did he know? Would he tell Pani Sowka?

He was quiet, and I kept my mouth shut. No need to add fuel to the fire.

He finally said, "I'll be honest with you, too, Anna. I'm not great with emotions, or with expressing myself. There aren't many people in my life who are willing to confront me, who aren't trying to get something from me."

A laugh sputtered out of me. This guy was too much. "Ken! I'm literally calling to take advantage of your plane."

"Yes, but you're admitting to it. And that's all you want, isn't it?"

"It is."

"The point is I like you. Very much. You're welcome to use my plane any time. There's no pressure, but...if you and Leo find yourselves drifting apart, call me. I'm here. I'd love to take you out, love to show you what I see."

Did this guy have any idea who he was talking to? Anna, the destroyer of lives?

Clearly not. He didn't know me. All he had was a projection of me he'd created in his head.

Still, this didn't diminish the fact that he was the only person in my life who still liked me. That and the fact that soon Oliver and Leo would be gone, my family would disown me, and the pain in my chest would still be there.

It couldn't be worse than being alone with all that. "If things fall apart, you'll be the first to know."

CHAPTER TWENTY-SIX

Leo

The flight to Mielec was remarkable. We got on the plane in Madison and landed only eleven hours later. I managed to sleep through most of it, and we landed practically outside Pani Sowka's door.

"Is this how the other half lives?" I asked Anna as we got off the plane. "No security, no layovers, no standing in line for thirty minutes to get an overpriced bagel and almost miss boarding?"

"I guess so." Anna shrugged. "Though it's not really the other half. Maybe the one percent. The other half of the world is far poorer than you."

I frowned. "Good point."

We caught a taxi to Pani Sowka's place and arrived with hours to spare before Oliver's bedtime. He squealed when he saw us, and I'm not sure if he was happier to see me or Anna.

It didn't matter. He was happy, and I'd never been happier. Anna said she was happy, too, though she seemed quieter than usual. I thought she might be tired, but she had slept for nearly the entire plane ride, speaking only when food was served, and even then she didn't have much to say.

"Just worried about Frankie." She flashed the saddest smile. It didn't reach her eyes and faded quickly.

"There has to be something more you can do."

She shook her head. "I've done enough damage."

We didn't get a chance to discuss this any further amidst the chaos. Pani Sowka was in a state I'd never seen, fretting back and forth, throwing things in and out of her suitcase, all while stopping periodically to stare at Oliver. Every time she did, her eyes filled with tears.

"You can stay with us as long as you want," I said. "And visit any time."

She narrowed her eyes, waved a hand at me, and barked a dismissive, "Ach!" before resuming her back-and-forth bag ritual.

My mom arrived the next day, which only added to the excitement. She was polite to Anna, mostly keeping her distance, and Anna did the same.

Was this some sort of woman code I wasn't aware of? Everyone was being so *nice*.

That evening, about an hour after Oliver's usual bedtime, we all piled onto the plane. Oliver fell asleep in Pani Sowka's arms, and she managed to get him into the travel crib without waking him up.

It was all going so, so well – until it fell apart.

We landed in Madison just before midnight. Oliver slept the entire time, and the rest of us managed to get a few hours too. He woke as we landed, a bit dazed to find himself in an unfamiliar place, but still jolly once he gained his bearings.

After landing, we met with customs and prepared to get off the plane. Just as we were about to leave, the customs agent returned and said there was a complication.

He didn't explain what the issue was, but asked us to wait as he sorted it out. Pani Sowka paced the cabin, taking the first opportunity she could to accost the pilot about leaving.

His answer was concerning. "They're telling me we need to wait for a manager from customs."

"Why?" Anna asked. "The customs guy just cleared us."

"I don't know why," the pilot said. "I'm sure it's nothing."

Anna's eyes, full of concern, met mine.

"What's wrong?" my mom asked, her head darting between us. "Why can't we go?"

I shrugged, trying not to betray how concerned I was. "They have to clear us. It's fine. Oliver needs to eat first anyway."

This distracted my mom and Pani Sowka well enough, but our peace was disturbed a short ten minutes later when an unannounced guest stomped onto the plane.

My dad.

Without even saying a hello, he started complaining. "I've been waiting in the parking lot for two hours. Why didn't you tell me you were here?"

"Sh!" Pani Sowka shot him a look. "Baby is eating!"

He put his hands up and whispered, "Sorry," before turning his eyes on Anna.

She stood and offered a handshake. "Hi, I'm Anna. You must be–"

"You're the wife?" He stood back, arms crossed. "Huh."

"Papa..." I warned.

"What?" He looked around for an ally, finding none as my mom was busy breaking down Oliver's travel crib. "I didn't get to meet you until now. I think that's strange. Don't you think it's strange?"

Anna answered him with a flat, "Not really."

He stared at her, his face twisting as though he'd smelled something unpleasant.

I let out a sigh. Why did he always come looking for a fight?

"Of course not." He nodded. "It's an easy way for you to make money, isn't it?"

"Papa!" I stood from my seat, shooting a glance at Pani Sowka. She was talking to Oliver, trying to get him to focus on eating.

I got closer, lowering my voice. "If you came here to make trouble, you can leave."

"This is the welcome I get?" He let out a huff. "If you have trouble, it's not because of me."

"Really? Because you look like the problem right now."

He stood back, looking me up and down. "My son the artist." He shook his head. "He *thinks* he's an artist, and now he thinks he's a father."

He was trying to provoke me. Provoking people was one of his hobbies, but I was too old for it.

I let out a breath. "All right, Papa. Take a seat. Do you want a drink?"

"It's almost midnight. We should all be sleeping. Who's drinking at this hour?"

Pani Sowka, with Oliver on her lap, raised a hand. "One for me."

My mom stifled a laugh, and I couldn't help cracking a smile. *What are you drinking?* I asked in my clumsiest Polish.

"Water, please," she replied.

I ducked into the minifridge and pulled out a glass bottle of seltzer.

"I know after you get bored of the kid," my dad loudly announced, "I will be stuck raising him."

Did he not understand that Pani Sowka was right there, terrified of leaving Oliver behind with anyone, even me? Especially me?

"Stop it, Papa." I took another bottle of seltzer and shoved it into his hands. "Have a drink."

"It's not easy being a father," he went on. "You can't just pick up and go partying. Those days are over."

I knew I shouldn't engage, but I couldn't stop myself. "You mean I'll have to be home? Like you never were?"

His face scrunched. "Bah. Stop it."

"I know how to be a good father. I'll do the opposite of whatever you did."

Anna let out a gasp, and everyone turned to look at her.

"Sorry." She sat down, eyes lowered.

My dad glared at her. "What's the problem with you?"

She shook her head, biting her lip and keeping her eyes down.

"Are you stupid or something?"

"Hey!" I said. "Knock it off."

He shrugged, smiling to himself.

"I might be a little stupid," Anna said, sitting forward. "It took me this long to understand what you've done to your son."

"Done to him? I haven't done anything to him."

"Right." She glanced at me, then back at him. "Other than abandoning him. Making him terrified of Oliver being abandoned, too. Or even..."

Her voice trailed off, and she looked up at me with round, brown eyes, as innocent as a fawn, seeing right through me.

I stared back at her. I knew what she was going to say. She was going to say I was afraid of being abandoned.

And she was going to be right.

A voice boomed from behind my sight. "Everybody get up."

I stood, turning to see two uniformed customs officers. One I recognized from earlier. He had his hands on his hips, his expression neutral.

The other was familiar, too. Tall, thin, pinched-faced.

"Passports, now." She pointed at Oliver. "And give me that baby."

Pani Sowka pulled Oliver closer and looked at me, eyes wide.

Nikki. She'd found a way to insert herself into our lives. I could hear Anna's voice in my head saying it was a nemesis thing to do.

"Hang on." I walked over, picking up my bag with the adoption paperwork. I pulled out the file. "Here's everything you need for Oliver. He's been adopted. Here's all the documentation."

"Adopted?" She raised an eyebrow, taking the folder from my hand. "By who?"

"By me."

She scoffed. "Likely story. Who's this guy?" She pointed at my dad. "Another Russian mystery?"

My dad hardly glanced at her. "A mystery to you, maybe."

"You think you're funny?"

Her voice was so loud she startled Oliver, his bottom lip trembling, threatening to go into full-blown tears.

Nikki started barking orders. "Old lady, over here. *Now.* You too, old man."

My dad shook his head. "No."

There could not be a worse combination of personalities. I stepped forward. "Let me give my lawyer a call."

"Get up!" Nikki barked, pointing at my dad. "And give me your passport."

He refused to look at her. "I will not."

Pani Sowka was not employing the same sort of willful disobedience. The color had drained from her face. She passed Oliver to Anna and stepped forward, holding her passport in her shaking hand.

Oliver quieted in Anna's arms, clinging to her fiercely, hiding his face in her shoulder. I watched as she stooped to pick up the bag with the travel crib, putting the strap over her shoulder. It bumped against the diaper bag, which was already on her back.

She then sidestepped until she had gotten around Nikki and behind the other customs agent.

I cocked my head to the side. What was she doing?

CHAPTER TWENTY-SEVEN

Anna

My family, excluding my dad, the stellar liar and window escape artist, is not known for coolness under pressure. My mom crashed her car once when she thought the police were following her, when actually they were stopping to get ice cream. Both of my sisters have burned chunks of their hair off when getting ready in a hurry, and Frankie blabbed his life story when arrested by the cops.

I am not an exception to this family curse. I am an overreactor, a panicker, and most of all, terribly uncool.

That said, I can't explain what happened next. Maybe I sensed things were going too well and my panic-o-meter, which likes to keep my nervous system at a low buzz, picked up on the trouble early. Maybe the moment I saw Nikki's petty, twisted face, I intuitively knew she wanted to inflict the maximum amount of suffering with whatever little power vested in her by the border police.

Or maybe my grandma was in my ear and in my blood, telling me that when the rules are stupid, we don't follow them – we find a way around them.

Leo's dad was a fantastic distraction, bellowing at Nikki about how he wouldn't stand up, he had rights, that he was an

American and he didn't leave the Soviet Union to deal with the likes of her, and so on.

This enraged Nikki, who resorted to grabbing him by the arm and trying to force him to rise from his seat.

In that moment, I saw my opportunity. Toting the diaper bag and the crib on my back, I hugged Oliver tight and quietly scooted down the aisle of the plane.

The other customs agent nervously watched Nikki's ill-fated wrestling match. I felt bad for the guy; he seemed nice enough. He hadn't given us attitude earlier, and had even tried a Polish greeting to welcome Pani Sowka into the country for her first visit.

How was he supposed to know Nikki had a hit out on us?

He was the last obstacle in my way to the exit. I got close to him, almost touching him, and mumbled, "Excuse me."

Without even looking, he stepped aside.

This allowed me to reach the edge of the cabin. Leo was the only one who noticed what I was doing, launching the occasional glance as he sifted through paperwork on the table.

"I have everything here," he insisted. "This is the adoption decree, here is his passport, and the death certificate of his parents."

Nikki paused her struggle with Leo's dad to walk to the table where the documents were spread out. "You know what this looks like to me?"

Leo put his hands on his hips. I could tell he was trying to contain his exasperation. "What?"

"Like you're trying to complete an illegal adoption. How much are they paying you for this poor baby?"

He blinked twice, then responded with his voice measured and slow. "There's nothing illegal about this."

"I've had this guy on my radar." She nodded toward her partner. "He has ties to the Russian mafia. His brother was a mafia syndicate."

"There's no 'Russian mafia,'" he said, voice raised to a shout. "That's not how it works."

Nikki swept her hand across the table, throwing the paperwork onto the floor. "Yeah right. I'm calling this in."

Her partner stepped forward. "I don't know."

"Do you want to work on night shift the rest of your life? Don't you have any ambition?"

He stepped closer and lowered his voice, though we could still hear him. "What evidence do we really have?"

"What more evidence do you need! He's *Russian!*" She threw her hands up. "Call right now and say we've got a Russian criminal. No one's going to ask questions."

"Yeah, but if we're wrong?" he asked in a hushed tone, his voice tapering to a whisper.

"Then the kid gets to hang out at the office for a week. Big deal."

Leaving Oliver alone, afraid, and in the care of Nikki?

I could envision him reaching for us and the heartbreak in his eyes when we didn't respond. I could see his red, tear-streaked face as she carried him away.

That was not going to happen.

My heart wasn't racing. My mind was focused. With four steps backward, I scooted out of sight, then turned to dart past the cockpit and down the stairs to the runway.

Oliver thought this was great fun, particularly the sound of the bags bouncing on my back.

"Where should we go, bud?" I whispered, looking down at him.

He smiled and clapped his hands oh-so-delicately, the sound as soft as the rustle of a dove's wings.

I looked up and saw my rescuer: a black SUV on the runway. A man stepped out and called out.

"Anna!"

I squinted. It was Steve, the driver who had taken me and Leo to this airport only a few weeks ago. "Hi!"

"Ken asked me to take care of you."

I could kiss him. (The driver, not Ken.) "We have to get out of here *fast*."

He jogged toward me, taking the travel crib off my shoulder. "I've got a car seat for the little guy, too. Ken's idea."

Ken's thoughtfulness was getting on my last nerve, but there was no time to think about that.

I looked down at Oliver. He was smiling, patting my face with his hand. "Let's go, little buddy."

• • •

The driver's first and only stop was my mom's house. (Did you know the first thing criminals often do is go to their mom's houses? Makes perfect sense when you think about it. Who else loves you enough to hide you from the police?)

My mom, dad, Frankie, and Lisa were slumbering peacefully until I came in, yelling my head off. I decided not to express my hurt that they'd had a family movie night and apparent slumber party without me, and instead told them what happened.

They decided not to bring up the whole me-firing-the-lawyer thing, instead springing into action.

Well, at least my dad did. My mom ran from window to window, shutting the blinds and yelling, "Are they coming? Are they here?"

My dad took charge. He told me to shut off my phone so I couldn't be tracked, then sent Frankie out to get a burner phone. In the meantime, he called relatives and strung together hiding places for me and Oliver until Leo's attorney sorted things out.

His calls were succinct. "Are you home this weekend?" Anna has to hide from the police with Leo's baby."

The conversations lasted no more than a few minutes, coordinating times and supplies. Amazingly, no one asked questions, such as what I had done, or why I had Leo's baby, or how Leo got a baby.

Lisa and I watched with awe. At one point, she leaned in and whispered, "Why is Tata a criminal mastermind?"

"I don't know," I said. "All this time I've underestimated him."

He caught our conversation, slipping his reading glasses to the top of his head. "You know, I'm not just a pretty face."

We erupted into laughter. Even my mom stopped running from window to window to shake her head – as much of a break from the tension as she could muster.

Within an hour, Oliver and I were on our way to Ciocia Ela's house. It proved to be excellent timing, as Nikki and a team of agents pounded on my mom's front door only an hour later.

After every nap, Oliver and I changed houses. We went to an uncle's house, then my cousin's apartment for the night, then, to be safe, my aunt kicked her boyfriend out of his apartment and had us stay there for the second night.

Sarah, who hadn't spoken to me since the engagement party fiasco, called and said she would personally come to pick me up and hide us in her house.

It was like something out of a movie. I thought we were doing all right until a picture of my stupid face appeared on the local news.

They said I was wanted for – you won't believe this – kidnapping!

It also said I was a Russian asset, which, come on. Rude. No one at the news station questioned a Polish-American woman throwing everything away to work for the *Russians*? Not even my beloved news anchor Dolly?

There should be more criteria to be slandered as a Russian agent in your community, but apparently, there isn't. Nikki had been right about that. Like bell bottoms, the Red Scare was just another retro throwback and I was the latest victim.

Thankfully, it took less than forty-eight hours for Leo's attorney to get in touch with Nikki's manager and show him what a monumental screw up her accusations were. The manager issued an apology and said Nikki would be placed on leave for her "aggressive imagination," pending an investigation.

My name was never publicly cleared, as the news moved on and lost interest in the supposed Russian asset, but still, I was grateful. The speed and seriousness which my family handled our predicament was something to behold. It might've made me weep if that was something I did.

My happiness peaked the moment I heard Nikki was in trouble, and plummeted when I realized the next step was dropping Oliver off at Leo's house and saying goodbye forever.

• • •

Pani Sowka and Leo's mom were waiting outside when I pulled up. Oliver was startled until he realized it was Pani Sowka crying and calling his name. He then reached his arms to her and she whisked him away, her cheeks covered in tears.

Inside, I stayed out of the way as Leo, his mom, and Pani Sowka fussed over Oliver. The boys were the only ones not crying, though Leo was close, his eyes red and misty.

Every time I looked over, I had to pinch my lips together to keep the tears in. It was better to stay busy with the work at hand, unpacking toys, mixing milk, and tidying as I went along.

After half an hour, the reunion died down and Leo's mom took Oliver off to feed him. Pani Sowka gave me a breath-squeezing hug before disappearing with Oliver's laundry (Ciocia Ela had gone a little wild and bought roughly two hundred outfits while we were in hiding, which were all now dirty).

This left me and Leo to stare at each other in the kitchen.

I spoke first. "I'm glad it all worked out."

"Me too." He looked down. "Thank you. What you did was amazing. Your whole family." He looked so tired. His eyes were small, his face unshaven.

Still so inexplicably handsome.

"We always get the job done. You know, immigrant labor." I let out a pathetic little laugh, then stood as my heart shrank in my chest.

"Do you want anything to eat?" Leo turned, pulling the fridge door open.

I shook my head. "I've got to get going. I'll just drop off this bag of toys in Oliver's room?"

"Ah, sure. That's a lot of toys."

"My family went a bit crazy, because they *are* crazy."

He laughed, leading the way up the stairs, down the hallway, and to Oliver's nursery.

I walked through the door and immediately saw how much more alive it was than the last time I'd been there. Was it because Oliver was in the house? Or was it something else?

There was a box sitting on the floor, a hole torn into one of the plastic sleeves, diapers spilling out. Toys overflowed a basket, and the shelves that were previously empty were now stuffed with books.

There was something else, too, something it took me a second to see. The walls, which were painted a soft blue before, were now covered in a mural.

The far wall had rolling hills leading into a town square. I recognized it immediately as Mielec, with the little butcher shop, toy store, and bakery Oliver loved so much.

The next wall had the Madison skyline, lakes framing the scene, with little boats and fish jumping from the water.

As it went on, the mural morphed into a forest with a castle in the distance. In the sky were two dragons, fiercely blasting flames on the trees below. I leaned in and saw there were people on the dragons – Oliver's parents, Dima and Agnieszka.

Hanging out of the castle window was Pani Sowka, with long hair cascading from a tower, and at the gate was Leo's mom, dressed in an emerald gown.

From the forest there was a trail leading to the castle. A beautiful angel with nearly invisible wings carried a baby, round-cheeked and perfect.

Oliver.

I leaned in to study him. He was smiling, mid-laugh it seemed, his eyes partially squinted. The angel had her arms wrapped around him.

I stared at the delicate shimmer of the wings, running my finger along the paint. Was that glitter he'd used?

I dropped my hand, my eyes finally connecting the scene in front of me. It wasn't an angel.

It was...me.

Leo cleared his throat. "I had a lot of spare time when you were in Poland," he explained. "I thought – I hope you don't mind, but you've been important to Oliver, even more than I knew at the time, and..."

I tried to swallow the tears, but it was no use. Two escaped, dropping down my cheeks heavy and fast. I wiped them away before turning to face him.

"It's beautiful. I know I've never told you this, but you're incredibly talented."

"I can draw a picture." He shook his head. "It's nothing."

"You sound like your father." I stared into his stunning blue eyes, trying to memorize the details of his face – the black eyelashes, the stubble, the half-smile. "Except you're nothing like him. You're already a great dad."

He stepped back, looking at the mural, his eyes scanning the sky and the castle, the rolling fields of grass, the dragons overhead. "Thanks."

It was time for me to take the hint and leave.

I reached out and touched his arm. "Take care, Leo."

He looked down at my hand, then back at me. "You too, Anna."

CHAPTER TWENTY-EIGHT

Leo

S he wasn't supposed to see the mural. I thought one day I'd point her out to Oliver and say, "You know that lady married to Ken Fielding? She helped get you here."

I followed Anna downstairs, trying to find a non-awkward way to explain it to her, but Pani Sowka appeared and started talking to Anna in Polish.

Despite my best efforts, I couldn't follow the conversation. Anna said my name, and I picked up on Pani Sowka saying the word "stupid," which I could only assume was in relation to me.

Pani Sowka gave her a hug, said a few more things, then headed up the stairs without as much as a glance at me.

Anna pulled on her coat. "I'd say goodbye to Oliver, but I don't want to upset him."

That was considerate. "Yeah. He hates when people leave."

Anna nodded, her eyes lingering on me. "I'm sorry about your dad."

"It's fine." I shrugged. "He's always just himself. I don't need him."

Now that Oliver was here, I didn't need anyone.

She smiled. "The lies we tell ourselves, huh?"

I managed a little laugh as the punch landed in the center of my chest, my lungs feeling like they were filled with shards of glass.

I forced a breath.

Anna looked past me, up the stairs, before turning to open the door. "Take care of him. And yourself."

I watched her walk to her minivan and get in, leaving me with the stinging smolder of her absence.

CHAPTER TWENTY-NINE

Anna

I n that moment, there were two things I knew for sure. First, I loved Leo with every ounce of my swirling, swelling, sputtering soul; and second, I would never see him again.

Why is it we don't know how we feel about someone until we lose them? We're like blind puppies, stumbling around, whining and crying at all hours of the night, peeing on the floor.

Okay, not so much the peeing, and I'm not nearly as cute as a puppy, but I was about as helpless. I drove back to my apartment in silence, then turned on the TV and sat on the couch, staring into the distance.

At some point, a show called *Know the One You Love* came on. The couples did not, in fact, know much about each other, much to the delight of the studio audience.

We don't always understand the people we love. In that moment, however, I understood Leo. I saw him, the little boy who had left his home, his brother, his father, and landed in a country he didn't know, surrounded by a language he didn't speak.

His offhand comments weren't glib. They were the truth. Leo rejected people before they rejected him. He didn't believe anyone stuck around when times got tough.

That extended to me – especially me. He didn't believe I would stay. He *couldn't* believe it, and he had to push me away. He loved me. I know he did. His heart ached for me just as mine ached for him, and I knew this just as I knew the birds sang in the spring and the fireflies floated through the summer grasses.

It was as constant and as fleeting as the seasons themselves. I'd never again get to feel his soft lips against mine, and that I knew, too.

. . .

Two weeks later, the world righted itself as quickly as it had turned. One bitingly cold Wednesday morning, Carl burst into the lab looking like Doc Brown from *Back to the Future*.

"They're going to create a tenure track position for you!" he said, his hair wild and wind-whipped. "We still have to hold interviews, but the position is practically yours!"

I thanked him for the news and agreed to go out to lunch to celebrate. I felt numb, and all day I waited for the shock to wear off so the overwhelming joy could take over.

It never arrived.

That same evening, Frankie got a call from his attorney saying the charges against him had been dropped. Frankie refused to tell us why or how, promising to reveal it at my mom's birthday dinner the following weekend.

At first, I thought he was pulling a prank. We'd resumed speaking since my voyage into hiding, which meant it was about time for the jokes to start rolling.

But it wasn't a joke. Before my mom's birthday, I caught a local news story debuting a video with "breaking news" in the case of the stolen camper.

In it, Frankie is seen coming out of his apartment building and standing by the front door. His bonehead friends pull up in the RV and get out to argue with him.

"Come on, we need to try it out. It's new," Jamie laughed.

Adorably, Frankie told them, "I'm waiting for my pizza," refusing to get in *three times* until they promised that they were "just going to take a spin around the block."

The spin that landed him in jail, without pizza.

Apparently, a neighbor had come forward with doorbell camera footage of the entire incident, proving Frankie had nothing to do with it. Brandon and Jamie, who did not get a chance to perjure themselves and seal their plea bargain, would be going to trial next month.

The whole family came for my mom's birthday dinner, and we all successfully feigned surprise when Frankie showed us the doorbell video.

"See!" he said when it finished playing. "I told you I was innocent."

"Frankush, we never doubted you." My mom grabbed his head and planted an aggressive kiss on his cheek.

Frankie pulled away, grinning.

"I had a little doubt," Lisa said with a half-smile.

He waved a hand, still grinning. "Yeah, right."

Though my mom hated presents, we all went in on a canvas print of a picture from the engagement party. It wasn't a posed picture – it was the one taken seconds before a pose.

I had my mouth open and my arm in the air, waving at someone to get out of the way. My mom was fussing over Frankie's shirt, Sarah had both of her kids wrangled under her arms, Lisa was grinning and pretending to take a swig from a bottle of champagne, and my dad was smiling straight at the camera.

The perfect chaos.

"I told you to stop wasting your money on me," my mom said as she tore off the wrapping paper. Then she gasped. "Look at this! It's beautiful!"

"It's the best thing to come out of Anna's engagement!" Lisa said, and everyone except my mom me laughed.

Lisa turned to me with a grimace. "Sorry. Too soon?"

It felt like it would never not be too soon, but that was the least of my problems. I was long overdue to tell the rest of my family about my sham engagement, no matter how painful it was.

It didn't matter if it got back to Pani Sowka anymore; she'd figured it out anyway. As I was leaving Leo's house, she asked where I was going.

"Leo and I are not doing so great," I had told her in Polish.

She looked at me, shaking her head. *"Child, do you think I'm stupid? I knew you were never together."*

I stared at her, and she went on. *"But he loves you. Believe me."*

Then she'd hugged me and left.

I would not be getting any hugs today. "I don't know how to tell you guys this…"

"Are you back with Leo?" Sarah asked.

"No." I swallowed. It was getting hot. "I have a feeling you won't be talking to me again for a while, so I'm trying to savor the moment."

Sarah stared at me, slightly narrowing her eyes. "What is it now? Are you engaged to someone new?"

"No…"

Lisa butted in. "Ken took her to a show at Fenway Park and I got a news alert about a 'mysterious, seductive scientist.'"

I shut my eyes. In my lowest moment, I agreed to go on a date with Ken, and a celebrity tabloid had taken the opportunity to broadcast a blurry picture of me in the crowd with Ken to the world. It was a terrible date. Once he had me, he had no idea what to do with me, other than show me pictures of his cars and his properties.

I'd rather the paparazzi had caught me eating an entire pint of cookie dough ice cream, or crying in the shower, or even the time I ran outside, pants-less, after the neighbor's dog got out and took off running down the street.

(These events all occurred during the last week. Except the crying in the shower. That happened every day).

"That was *you?*" Sarah's jaw dropped open. "I heard about that! The seductive scientist!"

"I'm not a seductive scientist," I said.

"Are you going to marry him?" Sarah grinned, elbowing her husband. "That'd be a party we'd be *happy* to go to."

He chimed in. "Put me down for lobster."

Everyone laughed, and I sat still, waiting for it to be over. Maybe they didn't need to know the truth? Maybe they could...

"Anna's engagement was not real," my dad announced, his mouth full of cake. "Leo paid her a hundred thousand dollars to lie to everyone so he could adopt his dead brother's baby."

"Tata!" I glared at him. "Did you have to say 'dead brother's baby?'"

He put his hands up. "That's what it was, right? His brother died, the baby was alone. Dead brother's baby."

I covered my face with my hands, and Frankie pulled one away.

"That was all fake?" he asked.

A table full of faces was gaping at me. I felt like the birthday cake, except no one liked me as much as the cake. "It was. I'm sorry. I really am."

"She did it to pay for your lawyer," my mom added. "*Both* of your lawyers. You should thank her."

Frankie turned to her. "*You* knew about it?"

She raised her chin. "Yes, and what your sister did was a miracle. You can't get mad at her. It's not allowed."

"I'm not upset," Frankie said, a smile spreading across his face. "I honestly can't believe you didn't tell everyone, Mama. Wow."

"That's the real miracle," my dad said, cutting another piece of cake for himself and lobbing it onto his plate.

The table erupted into laughter, and just like that, I was forgiven.

I guess lying really does pay.

My dad, however, was not ready to let the subject of my love life go. "I read an article about Ken."

I looked at him. "Oh?"

"It reminded me of a story Kurt Vonnegut told about Joseph Heller. They went to a billionaire's party, and Kurt pointed out to Joe that the billionaire made more money in a day than his book *Catch-22* had made in a lifetime." He shoved another fork full of cake into his mouth. "He asked him how it felt."

"I'm not getting the connection," I said slowly.

"Yeah, Tata, get to the point," Lisa said, taking the cake knife back from his plate to cut the skinniest, cardboard-thin slice for herself.

He went on. "In the article about Ken, they interviewed him about his kids. He has eight kids, you know."

I frowned. I didn't know that. I hadn't so much as done a single search on Ken. Not like what I'd done when I met Leo. Then again, Ken hadn't offered to hire me. He'd only offered to love me, or at least whatever version of me he'd made up in his head.

Ew.

"Three mothers." My dad held up three fingers. There was white icing on two. "His company created a machine that projects his hologram to read bedtime stories every night."

"That is...bizarre," Sarah said, shaking her head. Then she caught my eye. "Sorry, I mean it's cool. Innovative."

"Eight kids," my dad repeated. "So when Kurt asked Joe how he felt about that billionaire, Joe said, 'I have something he'll never have.'" He paused for effect. "'Enough.'"

Lisa tapped the end of her fork on her plate. "Still not getting it."

"You're saying you wanted four more of us?" Frankie asked.

"How many more of *me* did you want?" Lisa asked.

"Who would pay for four more babies?" my mom demanded, arms crossed.

My dad sighed. "You're twisting everything I say."

"I think I get it," Sarah said. "You're saying he's a billionaire because he can never get enough. Hence the eight kids."

He pointed at her. "Yes. You got it."

"Two kids are enough for me," Sarah's husband said with a laugh.

"That's because you don't have a hologram of yourself to take care of them," Frankie said.

"Yeah," Lisa added. "Because you're poor."

Laughter rolled through the room, and finally the subject moved past me and onto Frankie's chosen major at school – graphic design – which my mom did not approve of.

When everyone was done eating, my mom wrestled my dad's plate away and we started clearing the table. Despite my best attempts to tell my mom to sit down, she followed me into the kitchen, her arms stacked with plates.

"Don't listen to your father," she told me. "If you like Ken, then it doesn't matter what a hologram is."

I smiled. "What about the eight children?"

She set the plates down and waved a hand. "He can't have eight children. It's impossible. Your father didn't read it right."

"He probably did."

She stared at me, her eyes wide, nodding rapidly. "Okay. Okay. Eight? Eight."

"Relax, Mama. I'm not going to marry him."

She let out a breath and put a hand to her chest. "Oh, thank God."

"I'm not going to marry anyone." I turned on the water and started rinsing the plates. "Like you always said: you can't have it all."

She tried to edge me out so she could wash the dishes by hand, but I stood firm.

"Just let me–"

"No!" I hissed. "Go have some tea or something! Relax!"

"Relax," she muttered, grabbing a towel and wiping the counter. "You relax."

"I am relaxed."

"You don't look relaxed. Your voice is different."

I sighed, keeping my eyes on the pile of dishes. "How is my voice different?"

"You sound not normal. I can tell the second you call me. You've been this way for weeks."

I shrugged. "I'm fine."

"Aren't you excited about the job? It's okay if you decided you don't want it. You can go for something else."

"I'm excited." I took the stack of dishes and started loading them into the dishwasher. It wasn't used much. My mom normally stored bread in it.

"You don't sound excited."

I turned to her. "Mama. I'm just busy."

"It's not about having it all," she said. "Because you can't have it all. You have to decide what you want. You *get* to decide. That is what's so wonderful."

"I mean, not really. You always told me not to get married and not to have kids."

"I never said that!"

I stopped what I was doing to face her. "Yes you did! You said it all the time! I'm surprised you didn't get it tattooed on your arm."

She shook her head. "Tattoos are not nice."

Last Christmas, in this very kitchen, I'd told her I'd gotten a tattoo. She had demanded to see it, and I pulled down my pants, mooning her.

There was no tattoo.

I didn't feel in the mood to pull that on her again, though.

"Do you miss Oliver?" she asked. "I know how much you liked him."

I took a deep breath. "Yeah. I miss him."

"Maybe you can go see him?"

"The way you go see animals in a zoo?" I shrugged. "I don't think so."

"It's Leo, isn't it."

"No," I said as casually as possible.

"It is." She nodded. "I can tell. Your voice changed after I said his name."

There she went with the voice study again. "It doesn't matter what my voice does when you say his name, because he has abandonment issues and can't have a relationship with anyone. Except Oliver."

She was quiet for a moment, and I thought she might let it go.

But then...

"You know, Zuzia, I was not telling you what to do. I was saying you had *choices*. That's all life is. Choices."

Clearly, I'd made all the wrong choices. Why else would I feel like the world had no color in it and it would never be warm again?

"This isn't a good birthday discussion." I dried my hands. "Tata, where's the champagne? Mama wants to make a toast to you."

"Oh yeah?" he yelled from the living room. "What is she going to say about me?"

"That I thank God you didn't have eight kids!" she yelled back.

I smiled to myself and got the crystal champagne flutes from the cupboard.

CHAPTER THIRTY

Leo

The days grew dark as we entered winter break. I didn't think it was possible to get colder, but Wisconsin proved me wrong, encasing us in snow and turning our breath to ice.

It only made home seem cozier. There was laughter and rich food and toys that sang if you bumped into them. Pani Sowka stayed long enough to go Christmas tree hunting with us, and my mom didn't leave until my dad threw a tantrum about her missing his annual holiday party.

Even though my dad could be harsh, and selfish, and moody, he was still my dad. Over the years, I'd learned to keep my distance. I wasn't the ten-year old boy waiting for him to come home anymore, but Anna was right. I needed him, just differently now.

It turned out his little show on the plane had been intentional.

"I saw your Anna trying to get away with Oliver, and I wanted to help her."

My Anna. If only that were true.

I hadn't heard from her since she'd dropped Oliver off. It was only later I realized I'd never properly thanked her – not just for hiding Oliver, but for everything.

Every night, she appeared in my dreams. In one dream, we were in Switzerland, her face encircled by a furry hood, her annoyance at being forced to ski apparent in her smirk.

Another night we laughed and spun across the dance floor at our engagement party, hiding under the tables from Nikki.

In another, I watched helplessly from the courtroom as Frankie was found guilty. I called out to Anna, telling her how sorry I was, how I wished I could help, but she looked straight through me, her face streaked with tears.

If Oliver wasn't waking me in the middle of the night, grabbing at his cruelly emerging teeth, it was the images of her face lingering like a ghost in my mind. The night I had the trial dream, unable to fall back asleep, I started a painting of Anna. I wanted to reimagine her face like I remembered it – happy, warm, smiling.

That wasn't enough, though. The painting felt empty. I scrapped it and started over, this time adding Oliver in. I reflected his round little face in her irises, adding a glimpse of his chubby wrist that she loved so much.

Still, I couldn't sleep. In the early morning hours, the sun struggling to make an appearance, I decided to do something for Anna. Something to prevent that courtroom scene from coming true.

I didn't know what was possible. I suspected Ken, were he aware of the situation, could make it go away, but that wasn't my first choice.

Frankie's friends, Jamie and Brandon, were my first stop. It wasn't hard to find them. They lived in a swanky apartment with exquisite mosaic tile floors littered with red plastic cups.

I told them I was a reporter from a podcast, and I wanted to do a story on their case. I offered Jamie a chance to tell "his side of the story," and I *nearly* got him talking. Brandon, the more cautious of the two, got uncomfortable and told me to leave or be "forced to answer to" his dad.

I shook in my boots all the way to the police station. A polite officer took the time to talk to me, and I explained what I was trying to do. I asked to see the evidence in Frankie's case, and though he said no, at least he got a good laugh out of it.

I don't know what I was trying to find. Something. Anything. I went to the scene of the alleged crime, Frankie's apartment building.

There wasn't much there. Frankie lived on the third floor, and every apartment had a door to the outside. I went door to door asking people if they'd seen anything that night. No one even remembered the incident in question. It turned out the cops hadn't come out to interview people, either.

That fact blew my mind. I met a guy with a ground floor apartment facing the parking lot. He was Russian. At first, he didn't want to talk – he shut the door in my face. Then I explained who I was, in Russian.

Finally, my first language wasn't useless.

He cracked a smile. "You're the kid they arrested?"

"He's a friend."

He agreed to let me see his doorbell camera footage from that night and we ended up talking for two hours, long after I'd found what I needed. I ordered the guy a pizza, he brought out a case of beers, and by the end, he hugged me.

It had taken a strange turn, but the officer I talked to was happy to fetch the video and pass it to the judge.

Frankie walked. Mission accomplished.

So tell me — why wouldn't the dreams stop?

. . .

The next week, the students went on break and I took the opportunity to use my office as a studio.

Snow blanketed the campus, dampening any creature that dared cut through the biting wind.

I was an hour into perfecting the color of Anna's eyes. They were nearly there when a knock banged through the door.

I'll admit it. I jumped.

Before I could do anything, a figure in a long, black jacket with faux fur around the neck and arms burst through. "Leo. Hi."

"Mrs. Makowski." I must've looked like I'd swallowed a bug. "Hi."

Her eyes locked onto the painting and her mouth fell open.

Shoot. I should've covered it up, or turned it over, or something. "Just something I'm working on."

She took a step closer, her eyes scanning up, then down, then up again. "I guess you are not so bad at painting."

"Thank you."

"Can I sit?" She took a seat. "I'll sit here."

I turned the painting to face the wall and took a seat behind my desk. "How are you?"

"I'm not good at pretending," she said with a sigh. "I always liked it better here, in the US, when you go into a store and the person smiles, and they say, 'How are you?' They seem so nice. I still haven't learned how to be nice, even fake nice, after more than thirty years. I don't have it."

I had no idea what she was talking about, but I said, "That's okay."

"Frankie told me a Russian man gave the video to the police." She stared at me for a full ten seconds. "Do you know him?"

Ah. No small talk. Got it.

I took a breath and sat back. "I went to the building looking for answers. I bought him a pizza."

"You bribed him?"

"No, not a bribe. He wouldn't talk to me at first, that was all."

"Ah." She relaxed back into her seat. "So it was you. You found the video for Frankie."

I nodded.

She stood, coming around the side of the desk and putting her hands on her hips. Her coat was draped and long at the sleeves. I realized this must be the coat Anna had told me about, the one her dad called a flying squirrel coat.

I suppressed a smile.

"What?" she asked.

I shook my head. "Nothing."

"Are you laughing at me?"

"No." I paused. "Anna just ... she told me they call you the flying squirrel in this coat."

For a moment, she smiled, but then immediately turned serious again. "Why did you do it? Get the video?"

Her gaze was like fire.

I turned my head and looked out the window. "I felt like I owed Anna something, and I wanted to help."

I turned back.

Her stare was unbroken. "You owed her something?"

"And your family for helping with Oliver. That was incredible. You saved us."

Mrs. Makowski crossed her arms. "Anna says you have problems because you were abandoned. Is that true?"

I almost choked on my spit. "I'm sorry?"

"You were abandoned, and now you can't have relationships," she said matter-of-factly.

"Anna said that?"

"Something like that."

I shook my head. "I wasn't abandoned. I can have relationships."

She dropped her arms to her side and shook her head. "Then what is it?"

"What is what?"

"What is keeping you here painting Anna instead of going to her? Talking to her?"

I could feel her words echoing inside of me, deep inside the hollow part I kept shut off from the world. "Nothing. She's moved on with her life."

She sighed, her eyes narrowing to a glare, and I added, "Anna's with Ken now."

"Ken is not for my daughter," she said firmly. "She told me she misses Oliver."

My heart leapt. "Oh?"

"That's what she told me."

"Was this when she also told you I have abandonment issues?" I asked, cracking a smile.

Mrs. Makowski did not smile back. "This is why I don't like meeting new people. When you start looking, there are too many broken hearts. That's what being a mother is – a million little heartbreaks. Every tear they cry, I cry. Every sadness they have, I carry."

My image of Anna's mother was becoming clearer. She hadn't told Anna not to have kids because she regretted it.

Regret was the wrong word. Having kids meant a never-ending burden of wanting the best for them, worrying for them, being scared for them. Having kids was a never-ending burden of overwhelming love.

I knew the feeling well. "I'm sorry."

She waved a hand. "What is Anna supposed to do? Write it for you in the snow?"

I tilted my head. "I don't understand—"

"Do something!" she said, cutting me off. "If you are missing her so much, sitting and painting her, then go talk to her."

If I was capable of talking to Anna, I wouldn't be so good at painting. "It's not that simple."

She adjusted her purse on her shoulder. "Yes, it is. It's not easy, but it is simple."

"I thought you hated me."

"Oh Leo, you are so behind. All you men are such chickens." She shook her head. "Are you going to keep being a chicken, or what?"

There was no point in lying to the woman after she'd been so honest with me.

I took a deep breath. "I don't know."

CHAPTER THIRTY-ONE

Anna

Pain is funny, isn't it? As much as we hate to have our hearts torn from our chests, sometimes it's the only way to get us to pay attention.

I was finally paying attention, finally starting to ask questions. Why had I spent so much time butting into my family member's lives? How had they forgiven me so easily? And why, despite getting everything I thought I had wanted, was I so unhappy?

I had to build one of those solo submarines for a deep dive, dropping down, down, down, past where the light reaches, to where the fish don't have eyes and the squids grow until they're forty feet long.

Do you know about deep-sea gigantism? Animals that live thousands of miles beneath the ocean's surface grow to enormous sizes, and we don't know why.

Scientists don't know why, but I have a theory. Whatever you ignore will grow to monstrous size. The desires, dreams, and thoughts you shove into the abyss of your soul will only get bigger, until their demand for your attention crushes your ability to ignore them.

That was where I found myself: trying to escape the abyss, like one of those fish that deflates into a blob when you bring them to the surface.

It wasn't pretty. It never is.

That's another funny thing about life. Even when it seems entirely devoid of light, something miraculous can still happen.

I was lying on the couch, the pain in my chest a dull ache, when my phone rang.

It was Joanna, my dear, funny, brilliant friend from Zermatt, even though I'd missed two of her calls, even though I'd not written like I'd promised.

I started with, "I'm sorry I didn't call you back. I'm the worst."

"You're not the worst!" She laughed. "I'm just glad you picked up. I'm sitting at my daughter's basketball practice and have been dying to catch up with you."

We chatted about her work, the project they'd started, the funding they'd gotten from Ken. I admitted my shame — that I'd gone on a date with him — and she laughed so hard she snorted.

"What about your fiancé?" she asked.

I told her the truth, as much as I could muster at the moment. "Things didn't work out."

"I'm sorry. Really, I am." She sighed. "Are you okay?"

My instinct was to say *yes, of course, don't worry*, but instead, I said, "Not really."

I told her about the tenure-track job, and how my stomach filled with lead every time I thought of applying, and how my life had turned upside down because I'd refused to look within and had instead latched onto non-advice advice.

"What was the advice?" she asked.

I hesitated. "It doesn't matter. I took it the wrong way and never really thought about what I wanted."

"Knowing what you want is half the battle."

"It is." I paused, gathering my thoughts. "I thought I wanted to be a professor, a powerful career woman. I was going to focus on that – no husband, no kids. I thought it was the only way to be successful. The only way to be happy."

"Ah, and now you realize you hate working in academia?"

I smiled. "Not that I hate it, just that it's not enough. I'm not satisfied being a professor and nothing else. But I feel like I've worked so hard to get to this point, and to be a professor, that I can't have much else."

There could be no Leo, and definitely no little Oliver, who started getting ready for bed every night at six, long before I even thought about leaving work.

Joanna was quiet for a moment, then asked, "Have you ever heard of Kenneth Koch?"

Another Ken. I frowned. "Is he an engineer?"

"No, he was an author. He wrote a poem called *You want a social life, with friends.'* One of my mentors told me about it when I was getting my PhD."

"You read poetry during your PhD?"

"Mostly just that poem." She laughed. "It's about how you can't have it all."

My stomach dropped. This theme was following me around. "But you *do* have it all."

"Not really. I have what I need, and that's enough. You can't have it all. No one can."

My chest felt like it was under the pressure of the deep sea again. I took a breath. "Hm."

"The poem says it more beautifully, but my mentor summarized it like this. You have to pick two: a career, a family, or hobbies. Or maybe it was a career, family and friends, and hobbies. I don't remember, but you can only really have two. Not all three."

"What do you have?"

She sighed, not the deep sighs I caught myself heaving as I opened the empty fridge, but a whimsical sigh like a butterfly had just flown past. "Family is first, then career. I don't have time for hobbies, at least not right now. My kids are young, and I'm in the season of life where they need me the most. I love that they want to spend time with me. One day, they won't need me at all. 'See ya, Mom! Thanks for nothing!'"

We both laughed, and she went on. "Maybe when they're older, I'll work more to fill the void. But not before then."

"Your work is still amazing, though."

"It is, and I love it. It's flexible – way more flexible than what I could've had as a professor. I'm working part time." She cheered for her daughter, then added, "Every day I make the choice to put my family first. That means no late nights, no weekends. It took me a while to figure out what I wanted, and

I'm not getting promoted, but eh. I don't care. My work is still fulfilling, even if it isn't my whole life. I think that's the scam."

"What is?" I asked.

"Whoever convinced us that a career was all we needed to be happy. I mean, yeah, for a few people that's true. But for the rest of us, it's psychological warfare. They make it seem like if you're not killing yourself, you don't care and you're not dedicated enough." She blew a raspberry. "Boo on that. I still do amazing work. Just not sixty hours a week worth."

"So you can't have it all," I said.

"Wait, I take that back. You can have it all. Just not at the same time."

I covered my face with my hand. "Why didn't I meet you, like, six years ago?"

"I know, right? I'm so inspirational." She laughed. "I had no idea you might be looking for a job. We have a remote position opening up soon."

"Shut up. No you don't!"

"We do! Can I send you the details?"

The pressure in my chest lightened. I didn't think twice. "Yes! I'm applying! You better tell them nice things about me."

"I'll totally lie for you."

I laughed and got up from the couch. I could feel myself surfacing from the darkest of places.

I opened the curtains, letting the light pour in.

CHAPTER THIRTY-TWO

Leo

Anna's mom agreed to meet me again. She pulled a key out of the pocket of her flying squirrel coat, then yelled something at me in Polish.

I think she threatened my life.

...

There is no room for failure.

CHAPTER THIRTY-THREE

Anna

That weekend, Frankie wanted to take me to lunch to thank me for "selling" myself for his safety.

I told him there was no need, and I had *not* sold myself, but he insisted. At first, he offered to let me pick the restaurant, but after he balked at my suggestion of Five Guys, I agreed to go to a fancier Thai place in his neighborhood.

"I don't want you paying for this," I said, staring at the menu. "It's on me."

"Come on. I've got plenty of money." He reached into his jacket and pulled out a lime green grocery bag, dropping it onto the table.

"What is that?" I asked, peeking inside. I gasped. "Frankie! It's a bag of cash!"

"It's left over from what you gave me. I didn't have to pay the last lawyer that much. I was going to buy you lunch and give you the rest."

I shook my head and pushed the bag toward him. "Na-uh. That was a gift. It's yours to do whatever you please."

"It was for a lawyer," he said, pushing it back to me. "I don't need one. Take it."

I darted a hand up to push it back, but instead hit my water glass, knocking it to the ground.

Amazingly, it didn't shatter. "Sorry!" I called out, feeling the stares in my back as I stooped down to wipe up the mess.

Frankie laughed. "You're being dramatic. I can't keep this money."

A waitress appeared with a towel, and I used it to sop up the water. Once that was done, I let out a breath and took my seat. "It's yours, Frankie. Consider it my penance. I'm not going to mess with your life anymore. I'm not going to mess with anyone's."

His cheeks turned pink and he leaned in, his voice low. "I thought you were allowed to mess with family?"

I shook my head, standing as I took the bag from the table. I shoved it into his coat pocket. "You're keeping it. That's final." I sat back down. "I'll let you pay for my Thai fried rice, though."

He took *forever* eating – seriously, I've never seen him eat so slowly, and he then insisted on getting dessert *and* an after-meal tea. It was like the kid had never been out to eat before. Maybe jail had done it to him.

When I finally got back to my apartment, the sun was starting to set. The sky was cloudless, allowing the sharp red-orange light to blast into the building, bounce off the windows, and shoot straight into my eyes, blinding me.

I got to my front door and fumbled with the key, blinking over and over. I was either having a stroke or the sun beams had ruined my vision for the foreseeable future.

I managed to get inside and flick on the lights. Still blinking, I made my way to the kitchen and put my leftovers away.

When I got to the kitchen, I paused. Something smelled. I opened the fridge, leaning in and taking a deep sniff.

Nope, not that. The fridge smelled like the half onion I'd pathetically tried to save by wrapping in two layers of plastic wrap.

I shut the fridge and sniffed again. It wasn't a *bad* smell, like the onion that resisted all attempts at containment.

No. It was nice. Almost like fresh cut flowers.

Maybe I was having that stroke after all.

Was my face drooping? Were flowers a normal stroke smell, or was it just burnt toast?

I checked my reflection in the dirty window of the microwave, forcing a smile.

Perfectly average and symmetrical.

Was my speech slurred? I cleared my throat and sang out, "Smelly, smelly, everywhere, it must be a stroke!"

A laugh echoed back at me, and I froze.

"Hello?" I yelled, realizing too late that I was luring whoever was in my apartment to come out and murder me.

No response. I tiptoed into the living room, gasping at what I saw.

Every surface was covered in flowers. Vases with dozens of pink and white roses filled the coffee table. Hydrangeas burst from the corners of the couch and peonies laid on the TV. Flower petals dotted the floor, with sunflowers and marigolds overflowing the windowsills.

I gaped, mouth open, until my eyes settled on something on the far wall. I took a step forward and turned on the lights.

A canvas painting came into my view of a beautiful woman and baby Oliver, all cheeks and chubby limbs and smiles. I stared at the woman's face, my brain slowing to a halt.

I shook my head, trying to shake the realization free.

The woman was me, my hair in a wispy ponytail, a flower crown on my head. Oliver was mid-grasp, the joy apparent on his little face.

"Do you like it?" Leo's voice asked.

I looked up. He was standing in the doorway to my bedroom, his face partially shadowed in the darkness.

I pulled my hand away from my mouth. "It's breathtaking."

He took a step toward me, a smile on his face. "I was thinking of calling it *The Most Beautiful Woman in the World.*"

He looked, as always, amazing. His stubble was a bit darker, and the bags under his eyes were more pronounced, but standing there in his blue jacket, he still looked irresistibly cool.

I broke sight of him to look at the overwhelming number of flowers, taking a deep breath and pulling in the sweet smell of spring.

"What is this?" I asked.

"It's a thank you, for saving Oliver," he said. "For everything you did, actually."

I turned back to him. "I think I'm having a stroke."

"You're not having a stroke."

"How'd you get in here?"

"Your mom gave me the key."

I stepped back. "My *mother* gave *you* a key?"

A smile spread across his face and he laughed. "She did. This is, well ... my attempt at an apology, too."

His eyes. Those beautiful eyes. Pictures didn't do them justice. "Apology for what?"

"I've been having nightmares, so I've been getting up and working on this painting. It's what I see when I try to sleep."

I could have inhaled one of those rose petals and choked to death right then and there.

Luckily, I didn't.

Instead, I went for eloquence. "What?"

Leo got closer, taking my hands into his. "Like you told your mom, I have abandonment issues."

I sucked in a breath. "Listen, when I said that—"

"You were right," he said. "The moment I saw you with Oliver, how you adored him and how he adored you..." He shook his head. "I panicked. I had to get away. I couldn't let him get close to you. To me."

I squeezed his hands. "It's okay, Leo."

"No. I'm an idiot," he repeated. "I never should've let you go without telling you how much I adore you, and need you, and...love you."

Everything came bubbling up, leaving the squid and the submarine and the darkness, catching in my throat and pushing tears to my eyes. "Leo..."

He tilted his head, adorably biting his lip. "Can you forgive me?"

"Yes, you idiot." I grinned at him through the tears. "I forgive you."

He kissed me, setting off an explosion, his lips on mine, my heart soaring, my hands reaching, grabbing and pulling him in.

If this was a stroke playing tricks on me, I didn't care. I was floating away, lifted by the scent of roses, held firm in his arms at last.

EPILOGUE

Anna

L et's agree that if meeting, getting engaged, and falling in love don't happen in the traditional order, it doesn't necessarily mean it can't be perfect.

And let's agree that a dated Polish club, while campy and cramped, can serve as the perfect venue for a wedding if you are creative enough.

Or drunk enough.

Just kidding. We weren't drunk. Our guests were drunk – standing-on-the-tables-and-singing drunk – but not me and Leo.

We didn't want to have a reception. We thought it'd be more fun to get married at the courthouse and invite everyone to dinner at the house after.

My mom would not stand for that, just as Babcia couldn't stand for the ceremony not being at our church with a full Polish mass.

"It's taking longer to get through this than it did to get you to agree to marry me," Leo muttered as we knelt, side-by-side, in front of the priest.

"If you gave the priest a hundred grand, he'd speed it along," I whispered.

He turned to me, eyebrows raised. "Really?"

I turned back to face forward. "No."

Leo snorted and lowered his head.

Oliver served as the ring bearer, toddling down the aisle in his jolly way until he spotted my dad and ran toward him, demanding the chocolate he had been promised if he behaved.

Leo's parents both attended, and my dad challenged Leo's dad to a belly-measuring contest. (My dad won. Leo's dad laughed really hard.)

When we left the church, it was just me, Leo, and Oliver in the car. I was tempted to sneak off and get started on our honeymoon in Kraków early.

Leo had planned it all as a surprise, booking the three of us a room in the stunning medieval center of the city. Our room had a view of St. Mary's Basilica, and we could step out onto the cobblestone streets and weave between the pubs and cozy shops for hours.

"Shouldn't we get a head start on packing?" I asked.

"Nah," Leo said. "I want you to see the look on Nikki's face when she gets to the reception."

"Leo, I swear to—"

"Just kidding!" He laughed. "We have to go, though. Your mom told me she'd hunt me down if I didn't get you there."

"She knew I was going to run?"

He started the car. "Oh yeah."

"And you agreed to work with her? Against me?"

"She's scarier than you, so yes." He flipped his sunglasses onto his face. "Buckle up, Anna Doll."

I shook my head and smiled. At least in that moment, I had it all.

Glossary and Pronunciations

As my husband likes to point out, the Polish language is confusing and uses a bewildering number of C's and Z's (like the word szczęście, which means happiness, which is how I feel when he successfully says something in Polish).

Below are some words in no particular order with pronunciations (of my own creation) for your szczęście:

Babcia (BAB-cha) – grandmother
Barszcz (BAR-sch) – a Polish soup that can be red (made from beets) or white (made from homemade sour wheat starter)
Ciocia (CHO-cha) – aunt
Cześć (CH-esch, said as one syllable) – hi!
Dziadziu (JA-ju) – grandfatherZuzia (ZOO-sha) – a nickname for Suzanna
Kabonosy (KA-bon-oh-se) – thin, dried sausage made of pork
Kliszów (KLEE-shoov) – the village in Poland where my dad grew up
Kraków (KRA-koof) – a beautiful city you should visit
Mielec (MIEL-lets) – a city in Poland where my family lives
Pierogi (PYER-oh-gee) (plural) – Polish dumplings
Radomyśl Wielki (Ra-DOM-ish VIEL-kee) – the town where my mom grew up, and she'd like to point out she grew up in a town, not a village like her villager husband
Tata (TA-ta) – father
Troszkę (TRO-shke) – a little bit

Get a Free Copy of the Q&A

Join my newsletter and get a free copy of *The Love Payoff Q&A*, which will answer all (or some) of your burning questions about what parts of this story are fact and what parts are fiction. Pictures included! Get your free copy here:

https://mailchi.mp/d2d1e52df72d/tlp_signup

About the Author

Amelia Addler is the daughter of Polish immigrant parents who wanted nothing more than for their daughter to get a stable career and not end up a penniless writer.

Sixteen novels later, her mother is her biggest fan, followed by her handsome (and very American) husband. Amelia's books are available around the world, most notably on a shelf her father made in the family pierogi shop in Pittsburgh, Pennsylvania.

Visit her website at AmeliaAddler.com or drop her an email at amelia@AmeliaAddler.com.

Also by Amelia...

The Orcas Island Series

Sunset Cove

Sunset Secrets

Sunset Tides

Sunset Weddings

Sunset Serenade

The Westcott Bay Series

Saltwater Cove

Saltwater Studios

Saltwater Secrets

Saltwater Crossing

Saltwater Falls

Saltwater Memories

Saltwater Promises

Christmas at Saltwater Cove

Standalone Novels

The Summer Request

The Billionaire Date Series

Made in the USA
Monee, IL
02 September 2023

42044594R00163